But if there is harm, then you shall pay life for life, eye for eye, tooth for tooth, hand for hand, foot for foot, burn for burn, wound for wound, stripe for stripe.

Exodus 21:23-25 ESV

The Case of the Russian Maids
By John Köehler
with Timothy Choquette

Edited by Maggie Brydges
Cover & text design by John Köehler

ISBN 978-1-938467-10-3

A BEACH MURDER MYSTERY BOOK
www.beachmurdermysteries.com

Published by
 köehlerbooks™
an imprint of Morgan James Publishing

5 Penn Plaza, 23rd floor
c/o Morgan James Publishing
New York, NY 10001
212-574-7939
www.koehlerbooks.com

Publisher
John Köehler

Executive Editor
Joe Coccaro

In an effort to support local communities, raise awareness and funds, Morgan James Publishing donates a percentage of all book sales for the life of each book to Habitat for Humanity Peninsula and Greater Williamsburg.
Get involved today, visit www.MorganJamesBuilds.com

The Case of the
Russian Maids

A BEACH MURDER MYSTERY

John Köehler
with Timothy Choquette

NEW YORK

VIRGINIA

Acknowledgements

After writing two autobiographical books and a historical novel, crafting a murder mystery has been an entirely new kind of adventure. Whether due to madness or brilliance remains to be seen, though I hope a little of both.

Finding Timothy Choquette to collaborate with me on this piece has been a gift, as he added the spice and touches to make the story so much better than what it was.

Thanks to my editor, Maggie Brydges. I am humbled by her work and my lack of grammatical ability. And to Dave Potvin and Kathy Steele, who asked the tough questions and nagged me about too many (or not enough) commas.

To my wife Patty, who stood by me when I announced my lunatic idea of writing a murder mystery. She is always there, whether I'm writing or not, or the moon is full.

John Köehler

After I submitted a story to *Americas' Got Stories*, John Koehler asked me to collaborate on this book. He took me under his wing and helped me learn to fly. John, thank you my friend.

Very special thanks to the Muse Writers Center and their many talented instructors, for helping me hone my craft and giving me courage to write.

To my amazing wife, for mentally and emotionally supporting me through this whole process of writing. You truly are my best friend. Thanks to mother for the endless phone calls and never giving up on me. Without her support in the darkest days of my life, this wouldn't have happened.

Timothy Choquette

The hospitality industry (tourism) of Virginia Beach produces a large share of Virginia Beach's economy. With an estimated $857 million spent in tourism related industries, 14,900 jobs cater to 2.75 million visitors. City coffers benefit as visitors provide $73 million in tax revenue.*

This revenue is used to support education, public works and a number of local projects. The curtailment or reduction of tourists money would have an immediate and devastating effect on the city.

*Wikipedia

The Cast

Lt. Det. John Ordberg, VBPD SVU Unit, 41

Ordberg is a homicide Special Victims Unit investigator who uses a combination of logic, sharp intelligence and a dogged determination to get it right and bring killers to justice. He loves classical music and the blues (how he met Jameson). Ordberg is an impeccable dresser and lover of 19th century literature, especially regarding Sherlock Holmes and Det. Hercule Poirot. Born and raised in Richmond, he has a deep appreciation and respect for all things Southern, and the accent to prove it. He received a Doctorate of Psychology from Clemson University.

Officer Tonya Jackson, VBPD SVU Unit, 28

Working under the tutelage of Det. Ordberg in homicide, Jackson also works undercover as needed. She is a divorced mother of two, fighting her way up the ladder to the gold shield she covets. She knows the pimps and the underworld figures and relies on a network of snitches as needed. She is a loner and bristles under male authority, yet knows how to play politics well. She loves good wine, hip hop and is a kickboxing black belt. She spars with Jameson in the ring and verbally. She grew up in Portsmouth and received a Master of Criminology at Old Dominion University.

Private Investigator Rick Jameson, Jameson Investigations, 43

Jameson is a NYPD-trained detective-turned-private investigator who came to the Beach for a vacation and never left. Served with the Army Rangers during Desert Storm. His intelligence is based more on instinct and less on procedure, putting him at odds with Ordberg, who nevertheless respects Jameson for his success rate and often hires him for special cases. Jameson is a black belt in kickboxing, a surfer and plays in a local blues band. Dating Michelle Paige. Received a Bachelor of Arts at Columbia University.

Psychological Profiler Michelle Paige, 36

Paige is a psychologist and a part-time spiritual reader at The Heritage Center. While dating Jameson, she shared insights about some of his cases, and he began hiring her as an expert. She does onsite and evidence readings for Jameson, and also does casework as a psychological profiler for Ordberg. Studied Psychology and Religion at the University of Virginia, and also studied at the Edgar Cayce Foundation.

Investigator Mick Gorbach, Jameson Investigations, 29

Served two tours in Afghanistan with Special Forces targetting Taliban leadership. Sniper team leader. Honorable discharge after diagnosed with severe PTSD at end of second tour. Recovered and worked in law enforcement and security field. Now works for Rick Jameson. Fluent in Russian. Received a BA from ODU.

Nikolai Ivanov, Tsarina Enterprises, 53

Born in Moscow. After service in military, immigrated to the US. Runs Tsarina Enterprises, a transportation and employment company for young Russian men and women who come to the Beach every summer. He also allegedly runs a Russian prostitution and drug ring, enticing the prettier women to stay and earn big money. He is clever, has money and lawyers, and knows the right people. Received an MBA from Yale.

Virginia Beach Mayor Bill Stevens, 45

In office for ten years, preparing a run for Congress. Charismatic, good-looking and demanding. Made millions in the hospitality industry. A strong advocate for business growth and a supporter of the military and the tourism industry. Married with two kids, dynamic and allegedly enjoys relationships with other women. His wife is a divorce attorney and a strong defender of her husband. He will stop at nothing when it comes to supporting and promoting his city. Received an MBA in Business Finance from Cornell.

Craig Hansen, Hospitality America, 55

Billionaire CEO of the largest hospitality company at the Beach. Owns or manages ten hotels, including the Poseidon and several others along the coast. Single, rich and hotly pursued. Helped elect Stevens to office after working with him for years. Employs hundreds of Tsarina employees at his hotels and facilities. Received a BA from VCU and an MBA from Regent.

VBPD Homicide Captain Len Rogers, Second Precinct, 50

Brash, loud and the best Homicide Captain in Hampton Roads, with a stellar close rate. Gives his people room to get the job done and has high standards. Sloppy dresser, loves poker and spending time on his boat and attending local sporting events. Masters in Business from Old Dominion University.

VBPD Chief Walter Willie, 55

A completely political animal and a decent cop. Ruthless when it comes to keeping his city safe. Short, with the complementary Napoleonic personality. Nickname "Little Willie." Close friend of the mayor who is grooming him to be his successor. Friends with Hansen who is prepared to support his run for office. Daughter is reporter for local TV station. Masters in Law from Regent University.

Brandy West, Owner of Maxima Boutique, 43

Owner of a clothing boutique on Atlantic Avenue that caters to the rich and famous. Local girl with old money and social ties that run deep. Current love of the mayor, also dated Ivanov and Hansen. Advisor and protector of Ivanov's Russian employees, and allegedly involved as an unofficial madam for his call girls. Sharp, ruthless, will stop at nothing to achieve her goals. Studied business at Wharton.

George "Wheels" Johnson, VBPD SVU member, musician, 45

Lost the use of both legs in Desert Storm. Undercover cop and member of the SVU unit. Also makes money singing and playing sax along the Oceanfront's boardwalk. Served with Army Rangers during Desert Storm, where he met Jameson. Masters in Literature from Howard University. Teaches the Oceanfront homeless to read through Tidewater Literacy Council.

WAVY TV Reporter Kelly Willie, 27

Beautiful and charismatic, Kelly is a rising star at WAVY-TV, and hungers for the anchor position. Her Dad helps her by funneling inside information about crime and police biz, and Mick Gorbach does the same for her. She circles this story like a shark, while feeding the community titillating blood and guts info at every turn. She is taller than her father, and received a BA from William & Mary.

FBI Agent Elena Grigorevna, 28

Smart, fluent in Russian, weapons expert and a master of disguise and undercover work. Brought in to take down Ivanov. She is a fast mover in the Bureau. Born in Russia, moved here with family as a teenager. Father is a diplomat. Studied English and Russian at Georgetown University.

1

June 22 10:34 p.m.
Oceanfront, Virginia Beach
Alley between 23rd and 24th Street

TONYA WAS RUNNING HARD down the boardwalk like a tigress of pure power, while George sat poised and taut upon his steel chariot, stalking her from the shadows. Like so many times before, he wished he were running along side her. But that would never happen, so tonight he would take her down and teach her the lesson she needed to learn. Here where the seagulls flew and competed with the oceanfront sounds; people laughing, waves crashing and the drumbeat of his target's footfalls, rapidly approaching.

He had watched her for several nights now as she ran down the boardwalk after her shift ended. Never once a variation or change in her schedule; she was making it so easy for him. George knew all about her by now, after months of study; she the book, he the pupil. He knew about her loneliness and wished he could be the cure for it, the man who would be her one and only.

He watched her running, mesmerized by the sight of her. Her sports bra notwithstanding, her breasts bounced and beckoned in the moonlight and the glow from the many tall lamps posted along the boardwalk. He had seen men lust after her—how could they not?—but tonight she belonged only to him.

The boardwalk was still bustling with tourists, and the meandering people were a constant distraction as they made their way back from the bars and headed to their cars and hotel rooms. Noisy families laughed and played together, talking and shouting about the day and about what they would do tomorrow. He could easily listen in to their conversations (and did). These out of towners hadn't a care in the world about what they said—and often about what they did. They were here to have fun and fun they would have. He couldn't help but be amused by some of their antics, while also wishing they'd get the hell out of his way.

George grudgingly tolerated the whispers and giggles of the sauntering couples headed for their rooms, and sighed with regret as they passed him, for he knew they would share something that he would never have, as they wrapped their legs around each other and danced under sweat-filled sheets.

Regret pushed him farther into the darkness of his hiding place. He remembered the day his life froze in the desert of Afghanistan; the hurtling explosion and pain of the IED, the moment he was transformed into a broken creature. Fortunately his hydraulics still worked just fine, but he wasn't interested in women anymore, except for the one angel who could change his mind and his life and make him whole again.

His mind snapped back to the mission at hand, and he again became the lion he had been. He had done this before, on the hot sands of another place. His senses heightened to the point of supernatural overload as he watched her run north toward his position. He knew she was a creature of habit, and would turn and run through the narrow alley to cross over to the Jungle Golf lot where her car was parked.

He clenched the steel wheels that had become his legs and thought about the medals he had been given at his discharge ceremony. He had not placed them on his mantel or hidden them under his bed. They were beneath him, embedded in the seat of his wheelchair.

As she passed 22nd Street, Tonya picked up her pace and kicked harder against the concrete. Her stride majestic, she was closer now, so George slowly rolled back and tucked himself into the shadows of the dumpster enclosure in the alleyway between two hotels. The smell of rotting trash enveloped him, reminding him of the sick sweet smells of death, the smells of Afghanistan and the treachery, horror and brutality of his past.

With his black clothes, black chair and dark skin, he was a man of stealth, completely camouflaged and impossible to see, even for an experienced cop like Tonya Jackson, a decorated member of the Virginia Beach Police Department's Special Victims Unit.

She turned left—away from the ocean—and raced straight towards him, just like he knew she would. Once again he gave thanks to his God, the same God who took his legs and now was about to deliver an angel.

2

June 22, 10:36 p.m.
Boardwalk at 23ʰ Street
Virginia Beach

TONYA JACKSON'S BODY was on the boardwalk, but her mind was flying far, far away. She wondered how her babies were sleeping, and how great it would be to see them in the morning. She thought about the five cases she was working on, and about sacking out in her king-size bed when she got home. Since her divorce, the big bed had seemed so empty, and once again she longed for a man, his arms wrapped around her in the way she loved.

Tonya knew how to push herself to excellence through a punishing regimen of kickboxing workouts, yoga and, of course, running. Running alone on the boardwalk late at night when her shift ended gave her an adrenaline rush, and burned off her boundless excess energy, so that by the time she drove the few miles to her home in King's Grant she would sleep, just like her kids. All she wanted was four hours of deep, solid sleep. Please God, let me sleep well tonight, she thought.

She thought about her plan to make detective before she was thirty and smiled, because she knew she would get there; the youngest black woman to ever get the gold badge in a department dominated by white men and women. Her smile broadened when she thought about young white rookie cops taking orders from the black lady detective. That would be a fine day, a very fine day.

Tonya loved the feeling her Nike cross-trainers gave her; they launched her forward and gripped the sidewalk like Velcro as she made the sharp cut to the dark alley. She didn't fear the darkness and actually—after multiple street fights and shootings—she feared very little. Which would account for her complete surprise when a low dark form exploded from a hidden recess and took her down, hard, with a freight train of force.

She felt strong arms low on her waist as George lifted her up and over his chair, trying to break her fall. She instinctively tucked and rolled but the arms held on, and her back and head hit the wooden decking so hard that for a few moments she could not breathe, stars dancing in her eyes as her body tried to recover from the shock. She fought back from the rising blackness, and instinctively reached for her backup piece— the small 22-caliber Beretta she wore on her ankle—but remembered she didn't wear it when she ran. Damn!

Her life slowed down to a crawl of time while she thought about her kids and the graduations she'd never see, the gold shield that would never come. She knew she was going to die here in a dark alley surrounded by thousands of tourists who would not save her. She tried to scream for help as the dark shape of a man loomed over her.

"Got you!" said George "Wheels" Johnson, laughing down

at her. He let her go and rolled his wheelchair away from her. Wheels was also a member of the SVU and did undercover work, sometimes posing as a homeless musician. He was an excellent sax player, and the extra money he made playing went to his side job: working with the Tidewater Literacy Council helping people learn to read, including many of the homeless who inhabited the Oceanfront area.

Tonya lay still for a few moments and allowed her heart to slow, and her breathing to normalize, while she tested the various body parts that might have broken. She gave thanks to God that she was not in fact going to die, asked for forgiveness for what she was about to do to the man sitting next to her, who was still chuckling softly. She stood, slightly woozy, and had to lean against George's wheelchair handles for a few seconds. The dizziness quickly dissipated and she straightened up and stared down at the laughing man who sat in his wheelchair, (his "Stealthmobile" as he called it, all black titanium with racing wheels tricked out in chrome alloy).

He put up both hands, saying, "Now Ton, don't be goin' all ape-shit on me. Sometimes a brother's gotta teach you a lesson."

She took a step toward him, laughing, but he could see that her nostrils were flaring, and her eyes were narrowed, telltale signs of an impending Jackson tsunami.

He wheeled his chair backwards as she continued forcing him down the sidewalk. "Look, Ton. I did this for your own good. You been makin' this same run for four days. Bouncin' your booty around like a chocolate cupcake. All some crackpot gotta do is lay in wait so he can have you for dinner. Mmm, mmm, chocolate cupcake!" He chuckled at his own humor, and didn't see the running shoe that struck hard against his chest, sending him—and his chair—hurtling backward down the steep sidewalk, where it turned end over end and landed upside down on the grass median, wheels spinning and clicking.

"Damn, Tonya," he said, "I didn't even see that one coming. That was a good kick. Oh, cool, you gonna help me up... ow! Hey, that shit hurts!"

Several people had witnessed the wheelchair crash and rushed over to help, only to find Tonya further assaulting the poor man in the wheelchair.

"Hey, lady," said a large man with a prodigious belly and an I'M A REDNECK AND PROUD OF IT t-shirt on, "get off that guy, or I'll call the cops."

"Cops are already here," said the equally large woman next to him, as onto the scene rode two VBPD bike police.

"If you ever pull that shit on me again, Wheels, I will put you in a body cast! You'll have to trade that chair for a stretcher!"

At that, the two bike cops exploded with laughter. One said, "Looks like you met your match, Wheels!" Both officers mounted their bikes and headed north on the boardwalk, their laughter exiting with them.

"You cops are all crazy!" said the redneck. "You're not supposed to beat up handicapped people."

By now Wheels had pushed himself out of his chair, righted it, and leapt back in the saddle with a powerful display of agility and strength. He carefully pulled the limping Tonya onto his lap. They both began laughing, as Wheels slowly rolled the Stealthmobile back up the sidewalk.

"Wheels gonna give you a ride to your car, baby girl. Just hold on tight."

"Crazy people. Crazy as loons!" said the redneck as he walked away with his wife, excitedly planning how to post it all on Facebook.

3

June 22, 10:50 p.m.

104 Close Avenue, Shadowlawn

Virginia Beach

"YOUR BET, LOO," SAID THE HOST, Captain Len Rogers of the Virginia Beach PD, to Lieutenant Detective John Ordberg. The poker game had started a few hours earlier, after they had taken a run in his boat out onto Lake Rudee and then the Atlantic Ocean for a "case run" up the beach. The name was given by the good captain in concession to the time it should take his crew to consume a case of beer: about an hour.

They docked for dinner at Big Sam's, and rode back to the captain's house for the card game. Ordberg's good friend and ex-cop-turned-PI, Rick Jameson, watched as Ordberg considered his cards, and the stacks of chips arrayed before him. His card skills were legendary in the force, and tonight would do nothing to hurt his reputation, thought Rick.

Ordberg slid $200 worth of chips out into the middle of

the table. He looked at the captain, who had raised heavily during the hand. "I think I may regret this, but I call."

Cards were turned over to groans, while Rogers started cackling over his full house, reaching for the pile. "Hold up there, Capitano," said Rick, pointing to Ordberg's flush. "I think your bell's been rung, Len. Again!" They all cracked up as Ordberg deftly pulled in his chips and added yet more stacks to his growing pile.

"Son of a bitch!" yelled Rogers. "Bastard! I need to start giving you my money to bet for me. You're gonna clear us out of another grand tonight, John. Is there no pity in that evil heart of yours?"

"None whatsoever, sir, not when I'm working. But I do sincerely appreciate the gift of your money."

To much laughter, Rogers asked, "Saving for another suit, John?"

"Or maybe poker lessons for you, Len baby!" said Rick to another explosion of laughter. So the night progressed. All the players were experienced cops, white shirts, detectives or higher, active duty or retired, so tall tales were told about cases long since closed or new cases underway. And some that existed in the figments of their inebriated imaginations.

"Okay, I got one," began Rick as he dealt another hand. "Back in the early '90s a member of a Queens gang takes out some other dumbass member of a gang-with-no-name in a corner liquor store. No security cameras nabbed the perp's image, the owner of the store didn't get a good look at him, ballistics turned up nothing, and the few witnesses wisely refused to talk. This guy had a clean murder."

"No such thing as a clean murder," said Ordberg.

"Maybe not, but this guy got away with it, solid."

"Until...?"

"Until about five years later he got popped for armed robbery and sent up for five at Fulton."

"What's that got to do with the murder?" asked Rogers, checking his cards, saying, "Pass."

"Well it seems our boy had a fresh tattoo, and one of the bulls doing intake noticed."

Rogers was still feeling burned from losing the last hand. "Who gives a shit about his tattoo, Rick? All these assholes have tattoos. Shit, *you* got tattoos!"

"I've got a special one I'll show you later, Len." Even Rogers cracked up at that, and they concentrated on the hand, which Rogers won, instantly clearing the dark cloud hanging over the table. He lit a cigar and expansively motioned for Rick to continue with the story.

"So the dumbass with the new tat had the name of the guy he murdered, the location and the date, and an image of the liquor store from a photo he'd taken, all of it tattooed on his chest."

"A good attorney could still get him off," offered Ordberg.

"True dat, but there was one more thing." Rick fiddled with his cards, waiting for all eyes to turn to him for the story's climax.

"The Tweety Bird tattoo on your ass?" asked Rogers.

"No one's seen that but you, Len. Check this out: This dumbass had the tat artist not just put his name, but had him write, "I, Titus Jones, killed Rique Ingles on December 21, 1992.""

Several versions of "You're shitting me!" were offered.

"If I'm lyin', I'm dyin.' Dumbass got charged with murder and his tattoo convicted him. The judge added another 30 years to his ticket."

Rogers raised his beer and they all followed suit. "To all perps being stupid and making our jobs easy."

4

June 23, 1:40 a.m.

The Poseidon, Suite 2013

Virginia Beach

SERGEI WATCHED FROM HIS BALCONY as a young couple walked by twenty floors below him. The man had a prosthetic leg—obviously new—and he was using crutches to steady himself. Sergei thought the cripple was a pathetic waste of time and money, and wondered again why this country chose to care for cripples. As far as he was concerned, they should all be packed up and sent away, out of sight and out of mind.

A knock at his door interrupted his reverie. He smiled as he walked to the front door to look through the small round aperture of the peephole, which slightly obscured his vision. Holy shit, she was beautiful! He had picked her out of Ivanov's online lineup, the one you get to see only by knowing the right people, having the right amount of money and—of course—

the right password.

Her online picture had been captivating, but in person she was everything he wanted and needed; she was perfect. Her naturally blond hair was well cut and gently played against the top of her shoulders. Sexy bedroom eyelids revealed bright blue ocean eyes, while her full lips, with just the right shade of fiery red lip-gloss, completed the picture. He stared for a long time, becoming aroused, as she waited for a response to her knocking. He watched as she checked her phone, probably worried she had the wrong room or the wrong time. No – she was just in time, he thought. She knocked again, louder this time.

"Who is it?" he asked in his best Québécois accent.

"Debbie," she replied softly. Debbie my ass, he thought, smiling at her strong Russian accent. More like Delicious, Devine or Delightful. Regardless of her name, everything was ready for her, waiting only for the perfect queen to complete his tableau.

He opened the door and smiled at her. A quick look of alarm crossed her face as she looked into his eyes, but then she responded to his charisma and relaxed. He gracefully reached for and kissed her hand, turning her hand over to kiss her palm in an erotic way she had never experienced before. She shivered.

"Monsieur Magritte?" she asked softly.

"Enchanted, mon cherie," he whispered, his eyes still on her. "Please come in."

She walked past Sergei with a bold and self-assured manner, head held high like she owned the place because—truth be told—she had been in the suite before to clean it during the day, and twice before to service clients during her "night shift."

Floor-to-ceiling windows revealed ocean views as well as the 31st Street park, where a blues band was playing 200 feet below. The suite had been beautifully designed by the Poseidon's best interior decorators, and it showcased the finest Renaissance period furniture. The lighting was strategically placed and its soft glow illuminated the European artwork that hung on the fresco walls. The Bose sound system gently cast out a soothing wave of Mozart's concerto, "The Sparrow." The large two-room suite looked every bit worth the $1,500 a night price tag, and it was, but Sergei knew the sum was a small price to pay for a masterpiece.

As she walked to one of the Moroccan leather couches and sat, she imagined that a gentleman who could afford this suite would give her a grand tip, and she aimed to do whatever it took to get it. She needed just $500 more to buy the airfare for her cousin to fly over from Russia. Together they would start their new life, first as maids, then.... as businesswomen. She loved the sound of that word: businesswomen.

"What would you like to drink, mon amour?" asked Sergei, positioned behind the small wet bar.

"Rum and coke, please."

She walked to a table near the window, drawn by the items that had been carefully laid out: magnificent white swan wings, two tall cylindrical candles on floor sconces, and a large wig encrusted with strands of pearls and other jewelry. A full professional-grade makeup kit was sitting open, waiting to be used. Oh how she would love to have that for herself, she thought. Perhaps he will give it to me as a gift!

There were also smocks, a painting palette, several small crystal glass containers, an array of camel-hair brushes and a selection of the finest hand-made papers and parchments. His brushes were arranged in order, from the smallest of pinpoints to the widest three-inch fan brush. What precision he has, she thought.

She turned as Sergei approached with the drinks, and once again he noticed the way her hair brushed the soft flesh of her neck and shoulders. He wanted to taste her, and for a moment he was nearly overcome with the need to take her.

"You are artist?" she asked with a seductive smile, noticing his desire. "What do you paint?"

"Tonight, my dear," he replied, "I will paint you."

She clapped her hands with delight and took the glass and raised it up to his. As the crystal glasses met, the purest "C" note was formed, melding with the soft wave of Mozart's concerto. They smiled and looked into each other's eyes, both anticipating the art about to be created.

5

June 23, 10:40 a.m.

VBPD, Second Precinct HQ

Virginia Beach

"I DON'T GIVE A FLYING FUCK if he's about to leave on vacation, the shit's going down here, Martin! Yeah, I already told you it was the Poseidon. Did I stutter? I want all hands on deck. Yeah, we already got a team there, been there for an hour until Ordberg's team gets there. Okay, are we good? Do you understand the words coming out of my mouth? Good, now get it done!"

VBPD Second Precinct Capt. Len Rogers slammed the phone down. As his anger rose, so did he. He grabbed an unlit cigar, bit the end off and spit it into the trash. He paced like a caged animal waiting to be fed, and kept his team on hold while he ticked off all possible detectives and uniforms he could put on this case—a case that could make – or ruin – his career. Murder at the Poseidon. Damn!

Rogers was considered a good cop and an excellent administrator, had put in the time and hefted his bones all the way up the ladder. He could growl and snap like a junk-yard dog, but was also known for giving praise where praise was due, keeping his people happy and backing them up—always.

He sat down at the conference table and loosened his tie; sweat poured off his face, irritating him even more. He looked at the perfectly dressed, non-sweating Lt. Detective John Ordberg, head of SVU. It irritated Rogers that Ordberg never sweated, never seemed flustered and never ever was improperly attired.

Today the "proper attire" was a beautifully cut, light gray Luciano Barbera suit, with a Calvin Klein shirt, a Corsini tie and matching pocket square. He looked like a dandy, but truth is, thought Rogers with some jealousy, he looked like he belonged on the cover of *GQ*.

Rogers reached across the table and fingered Ordberg's jacket lapel. "Italian, right John? You should buy stock at Beecroft & Bull, as much as you spend there. How the heck do we pay you enough for these kinds of clothes?"

"You don't," replied Ordberg, as he flicked an invisible dust ball from his lapel.

"See, what did I tell you guys," Rogers said, turning to the others. "The Loo is dipping into the local card games and running numbers!" The team laughed, by now used to the friendly banter between their Captain and Lieutenant.

"I do not dip, Captain, as you well know. I have, however, been known to win at cards, for which I must sincerely apologize for your losses last night. Perhaps you should not bluff so often, sir, or at least try not twitching your left eyebrow so much. I will be visiting Craig Beecroft soon, thanks to you, sir, and I shall give him your kind regards."

"You're an asshole, Ordberg, but you're my asshole!" said the Captain with a smile. He turned to the assembled SUV crew—his best—consisting of Ordberg, Detective Bobby Brown, two plainclothes detectives borrowed from Homicide, Special Officer Jackson and Wheels. He looked hard at Jackson, noting her black eye and bruised arms.

"Holy shit!" said Rogers with a feigned look of surprise. "Someone finally took down the mighty Jackson. Say it ain't so, Tonya. Tell me you tripped and fell carrying those two babies down for breakfast. Tell me it wasn't some cripple in a wheelchair."

To the subsequent laughter from the team, and with a sharp look at Wheels, Tonya replied, "You know what happened, Captain."

"Oh, I know what happened alright. Wheels here took you out like a bad date. Heard he was laughing the whole way. My bike guys are telling some mighty big stories with the headline: "Kickbox Queen Killed by Cripple." News at eleven!"

The room exploded with laughter.

"Why did you call us in, sir?" asked Ordberg.

Rogers stared at him for a beat. "John, we got a bad one here, a homicide down at the Poseidon. Looks like one of your Russian girls worked her way up from maid service to a call girl. There's a bad scene there, never heard anything like it. The hotel staff is freakin' out, plus I got the chief and the mayor already going ballistic, mainly 'cause that asshole Craig Hanson is pulling their strings and talking about a shutdown of the tourism industry, abuse of his employees, blah blah blah."

He paused and looked at the team members, settling on Ordberg. "Here's what the mayor is really worried about, John. The media is having a feeding frenzy. There's three broadcast trucks on site already, and the Chief doesn't want to see this shit on CNN. We gotta clear the scene ASAP and put this thing to bed. I want this piece of shit found and behind bars, and I want it now. Is that clear, Ordberg?"

"Yes, sir, imminently clear," said Ordberg, rising from his chair.

"Then get your asses down to the scene, and get it right."

Ordberg paused on the way out with his team, and turned back to the Captain. "I may need to call in some special help on this one, sir."

"Yeah, I already cleared that with the chief. You get whatever you need, special budget, the whole nine yards, just save your receipts. And no, you can't buy a new suit and turn a slip in, you hear me? As for personnel, get whoever you need."

"You know who I want, sir."

"Yeah, you want that asshole Jameson, and his Tarot card mentalist. What's her name...Paige!"

"Sir, we do not hire her for her readings, though that might be wise. But, in fact, she is a Doctor of Psychology, as you well know, and we hire her to establish a psychological profile of the killer. This is precisely the way that Holmes solved his cases, sir. Take for instance the classic solution from the *Hound of the...*"

"Don't start that Sherlock shit with me, Loo! Just get down there and get it done."

6

June 23, 11:00 a.m.

Poseidon lobby

Virginia Beach

ORDBERG SPED UP THE POSEIDON'S parking garage ramp, taking rumble strips at high speed. He pulled into a handicapped space near the pedestrian bridge to the Poseidon and slammed on the brakes so hard the entire team bounced in their seats like bobble-head dolls.

"Damn, Loo," said Rick from the backseat, "NASCAR needs you."

They grabbed their gear, checked their weapons and exited the black Suburban Capt. Rogers had finagled from the budget last year. As they crossed the Poseidon's second-floor overhead bridge they looked down at the large crowd on the sidewalk. A WAVY-TV reporter was doing live interviews, and the crowd spilled onto Atlantic Avenue, where traffic was bumper-to-bumper for three blocks in either direction.

"They look like piranhas waiting to feast," quipped Tonya, pointing down at the news team.

"Yeah," replied Rick, "They're attracted to blood. Welcome to the Amazon!"

Ordberg sent his team up to the murder scene and walked down the stairs to the lobby and flashed his gold badge at the startled desk agent.

"Lt. Detective Ordberg to see your manager, please."

"Right this way, sir, he's expecting you," replied the agent, and led Ordberg to a second-floor corner office overlooking the boardwalk, richly appointed with mahogany bureaus, Queen Anne furniture, Persian carpets and several original Disney animation cells.

"Mr. Pratt," said the desk agent to the man rising from behind the desk, "This is officer Orbit."

"Actually," said Ordberg as the agent left the room, "I am Lieutenant Detective John Ordberg of the Special Victims Unit. Pleasure to make your acquaintance, Mr. Pratt. I see you're a collector," he said, gesturing to the prints.

"Forgive my staff, lieutenant," remarked Pratt. "We've never had a murder before and we're all quite shaken up. Especially the maid who found the body."

"Is she still here?"

"Of course. I knew you would need to speak with her."

"Thank you. I'm afraid your hotel is in lockdown as of this moment. Since it's a crime scene, we must interview every guest."

Pratt turned red and began speaking and choking at the same time. "But that's not possible! We have over 300 guests staying here at the moment. This is a 4-star hotel with some *very* important guests, and we can't just ask them to stay put in their rooms."

"I agree. Tell them to stay in the hotel proper, which includes your pools, the terrace, restaurants and lounges. We should have the interviews wrapped up within 24 hours."

"24 hours! Are you out of your mind?! Because if you *want* chaos and pandemonium, that will do it! No, absolutely not. Let's see if we can settle this, lieutenant." He reached for his phone and dialed a number. "Margie, get me Mr. Hansen on the line.... Great, I'll be waiting for the call."

He slammed the phone down—eyeing Ordberg—and wondered how much money his hotel would lose because of the murder. There goes my bonus, he thought. His phone rang, and he quickly explained to Craig Hansen, CEO of Hospitality America—the largest hotelier at the Beach—what had happened. He listened intently for a few moments, rang off, and appraised the lieutenant.

"Lieutenant, you can expect a call very shortly." With that he spun his chair around and began working on his computer.

Within a few minutes Ordberg's phone rang, with the Second Precinct phone number displayed on the caller ID. He knew this would not be a good call.

After listening to a few seconds of Captain Rogers exploding through the phone, Ordberg held it away from his ear, periodically repeating, "Yes, sir." Pratt turned around and smiled smugly. Finally Ordberg ended the call and stood. Pratt followed suit.

"I beg your pardon, Mr. Pratt," said Ordberg. "We will not be interviewing all your guests after all. But I will need all your security tapes from yesterday and this morning, your financial and booking reports for this week, and of course we will need to interview all your staff, and I do mean *all* of them, Mr. Pratt. Is that agreeable?"

"I'll personally take care of it, Lieutenant."

"Excellent. And would you be so kind as to have your security team keep all the press outside of the building?"

"With pleasure."

As he was walking out, Ordberg turned and gestured to one of the prints. "An original cell from Walt Disney's *Pinocchio*. Hmmm, this was later in the film, so I'm going to say this cell was painted circa 1939, with a value of $4,500. Would that be about right, Mr. Pratt?"

Pratt stared at Ordberg for a beat, and nodded his head. Ordberg smiled, shot Pratt a two-fingered Boy Scout salute, and headed for the elevator.

7

June 23, 11:22 a.m.

The Poseidon, room 2013

Virginia Beach

AS THE BRUSHED STEEL GATES of the elevator doors opened, Ordberg stepped out onto the 20th floor, the stench of vomit assaulting his nose. Two rookie cops—the first to arrive on the scene over an hour ago—stood outside room 2013 with shocked expressions on their faces. One looked rather lime green and—judging by the stain on his uniform— was the source of the smell.

"Loo," they both said, raising their hands in half salutes. Ordberg nodded at both and walked into the suite.

It looked like a scene courtesy of Jack the Ripper, had it been another time and place. His eyes were drawn to the bed and the tableaux that had been arranged around it. Two tall cylindrical candles positioned on either side of the bed were still lit. Pools of paraffin overflowed their crystal sconces and continued to splash onto the fine red oak nightstands.

Two pure white swan wings were nailed to the wall on either side of the bed. As the smoke rose it graced their wings and suggested the flight they once had. Upon the wall, a beautiful landscape had been painted in reddish brown paint just above the headboard, extending the full width of the bed. There were splatters of violence on both sides of the mural, as if in grisly homage to Jackson Pollock.

"It would seem we have an artist," said Orberg to his team. "A performance artist."

"He must have bound her, stood her up, and cut her throat," said Rick Jameson, part of the 3-person team from Jameson Investigations. "He did some splatter work, then he drained her into that container, and painted the landscape with her blood. This is a very sick dude, John."

The victim lay spread-eagled on her back with her arms and legs tied to the bedposts of the king-sized bed. Large pillows had been positioned underneath to prop up her frame. She was completely naked, a horrified look on her face, staring at the landscape painted with her own blood. Rope bracelets were still knotted around her wrists, the redness of the flesh proving her struggle for freedom. She was exquisitely beautiful and her body was perfect: large, firm breasts and an hourglass shape that would have done justice to any men's magazine. On her head was a wig that was nearly three feet high, with ropes of pearls and other adornments entwined through it.

He had decorated her with a heavy white foundation on her face and neck, along with excessive aromatic powder that was dusted on her wig. Her lips were painted a bright scarlet red, matching the gaping cut that ringed her neck—from one ear to the other—and so deep that her spine could be seen.

Next to the body was a note, which seemed to be written on some type of vellum paper, based on its uneven texture and color, expensive paper meant to look old. The note had been written in a beautiful, cursive hand. It seemed to harken from another, more formal and elegant era.

"Very well," said Ordberg after digesting the setting, "Let us remember this scene. Burn it into your minds. Jackson, did you get some footage? Good. Now, what do we know about our dearly departed?"

Jackson consulted her iPhone. "Her name was Natasha Lischininsky, 23. Employed by Tsarina Enterprises as a maid in this hotel. Let's see.... says she comes from a place in Russia called Osorgino. I have no idea where that is."

"It's a suburb of Moscow," offered Gorbach.

"Looks to me," said Jameson, "she was doing a whole lot more than maid service. Micky, can you get us a meet with our favorite Russian? Let's see what Mr. Ivanov has to say about one of his employees turning up naked in a hotel."

"Naked and *dead*, Rick. Naked and dead."

"Talk to me, Rick," said Ordberg with a baton twirl of his hand. "What does your gut say?"

"It says I'm hungry for some lunch, Loo. I'm thinking sushi and you're buying."

"All in good time, my gastronomic snob. In the meantime, tell me what you think about the perp."

"It wasn't about the sex," said the petite woman standing next to Jameson. Michelle Paige was a psychologist hired by Jameson and the VBPD to help build a profile on tough cases. Her practice was located at the Heritage Center near the North End of the Beach. There she treated clients with a blend of traditional psychology and various types of homeopathic and holistic healthcare, dream interpretation, prayer and spiritual readings. All of which was—according to Rogers—total bullshit.

Ordberg motioned for her to continue.

"Even if he had sex with her, he really wanted to dominate her, to teach her—and us—a lesson. I think this entire tableau is a personal message. This guy is sharp; an intellectual *and* a sociopath. He cares only for himself though perversely, he believes he's a good and caring man. He wants to bring order to the world. But I think something happened to him—with his mother or his father. I see real hatred here."

Ordberg clapped quietly for effect.

"A bottle of Dom Perignon for Ms. Paige. Well done, Michelle. We are in fact looking at a scene conjured up by a vile—but brilliant—mind, a sociopath indeed. One who does not care about the people around him. It reminds me of *The Adventure of the Blue Carbunkle*, but that's for another day. The wig is interesting. Jackson, would you mind sending that over to Tom Tom and see what he can tell us. Make sure you mention the smell of the powder. Intriguing."

"On it," said Jackson, and in moments she had whipped out her iPhone, snapped three photos and emailed them to Professor Tom Thomlin, nicknamed Tom Tom. He was a professor of History & Literature at Regent University, and a police advisor and expert on historical forensics, including art and literature. Jackson dialed his number.

"Hi, Tom Tom...yeah, I know you're teaching, but we got a hot one. Did you get the email? Uh-huh. Yeah. Okay, you're sure? Thanks, we owe you another one."

She hung up her phone and announced, "Tom Tom says this looks like a scene from *Daphne and Chloe*, by Jack Openbook."

"Jacques Offenbach," said Ordberg. "Rather obscure, but

it does fit the timeframe of the mid-18th century." He stared at the scene a while longer, rubbing his chin, as the forensics team continued to work their magic. "But what is the message of the entire set, wig and the makeup?"

"Love is art," said Wheels Johnson, rolling his chair into the room, a VBPD badge hanging from a lanyard around his neck.

"Well, well, well," said Jameson. "Look who just rolled in, someone who likes sushi!"

The team backed farther away as the technicians photographed, sketched, dusted and videotaped the scene from multiple angles. They were good at what they did, and took their time, knowing how important their efforts would be later during trial, where evidence is king. A botched job at the murder scene could kill a case faster than a speeding bullet.

One of the techs carefully bagged the note in a clear Ziplock bag and brought it to Ordberg, saying, "Here, sir. Please be careful. We have to run it through the lab, so I'll need it back. It's a very interesting paper, very thick yet supple, almost like thin leather."

"Parchment, I should guess," replied Ordberg. "It was made from the cured skin of an animal before the invention of the printing press to record important documents. This could be quite old. Thank you, Mark, we will return it in good shape."

The others gathered around to examine the document.

It read:

> *Salutations my friends,*
>
> *When you gaze upon the scene of my masterpiece you will understand the magnificence of my work.*
>
> *I am sharing with you and the world the grandest display of life.*
>
> *The candles are lit and her wings will take flight to immortality.*
>
> *I have covered the blood of her sins with pure white perfection and given her back everything she has lost.*
>
> *Now she lives forever as a great piece of art, a masterwork of life and death.*
>
> *Now she gazes at the seventh wave and the incoming tide. My beautiful ballerina has been restored to Excellence.*
>
> *Sergei*

"Holy shit!" exclaimed Rick, "this asshole commits murder and acts like he's Michelangelo, God's gift to art."

"More like Jackson Pollock if you ask me," offered Wheels.

"Or maybe both," injected Ordberg. "Michelangelo represents the classical, whereas Pollock is a purely modern anti-representational, contemporary. Here we have opposing versions, contrasted side-by-side. The brush painting is quite disciplined, painted in a classical style, clearly by someone who's had training. Even the splatter work is done with a focus."

"But how can he call this art?" asked Rick. "Does he really think what he's done here is a piece of art?"

"He absolutely thinks what he's done is art," said Michelle, walking closer to the painting. "But you have to remember that the entire room and the victim is part of his artwork."

She pointed to the candles and other decorations. "This man—and we can be quite certain that this is a man based on the behavioral evidence—is obviously conflicted. He loves women and projects an old-fashioned adoration through what he's added to the room, not to mention the painting."

She pointed to the splatter work on the walls and continued. "Here we see the rage of a wronged man, possibly wronged at some point by a woman from his past. He sees his rage as an expression of love, and a necessary balancing of his past with his present. To him, killing the woman is an act of love and an expression of his life. Classic sociopath."

"So he just doesn't care?" said Jackson.

"Oh, he cares deeply," answered Michelle. "He just cares too much about some things and not at all about others."

"Good," said Ordberg, "Now we have work to do downstairs. Jackson, you, Johnson and Mick take one of the uniforms—the clean one I should think— and get the security tapes, along with computer records of all transactions done in the past month. They may not let us interview the guests, but they will provide the records. If they give you any guff, let me know."

"Guff?" said Rick. "What kind of word is 'guff?' Seriously, who uses words like that, other than Sherlock Holmes? Loo, the proper word would be 'shit.' You meant to tell Jackson 'if they give you any shit, let me know.'"

"Thank you Richard. I shall endeavor to sink more often to your level: Cro-Magnon."

"So what about the staff interviews, you want me to work on those?"

"No, I think our two borrowed homicide detectives and their team can handle those, along with the other bodies the good captain is sending over. You and Michelle are going to assist me with the interview of the maid who found the body. Apparently she knew the vic. Small world indeed."

"What about the sushi, Rick?"

"After the interview, John. First fame, then food."

They returned to the lobby and looked out to the sidewalk, where the crowd of tourists and news crews milled about, with Poseidon security keeping a wide aisle open leading up to the doors for guests.

"I'm going to go feed the sharks," offered Ordberg to the others, "I'll meet you back here in a few minutes." He headed out the front door and into the maelstrom.

"Lieutenant Ordberg!" shouted Kelly Willie, a reporter with WAVY TV.

Willie was young, pretty and had killer instincts. She was working hard to fight her way up to a coveted anchor position before she was thirty. It helped that her father was none other than Walter Willie, Virginia Beach's chief of police. Ordberg approached her and assumed the position as she pulled her microphone wire—and her cameraman—into position while the crowd moved in expectantly.

"This is Kelly Willie reporting live outside the Oceanfront Poseidon with Lieutenant John Ordberg from the Virginia Beach Police Department's Special Victims Unit. Lieutenant, what can you tell us about the murder?"

"Early this morning a young woman was murdered in one

of the rooms at the Poseidon. We're investigating the crime and hope to have it solved quickly."

"Is it true the victim was dressed up in a macabre way and her blood was used in a painting by the murderer?"

Ordberg paused a beat and stared at the young reporter. How could she possibly know that already? Was it her daddy, or a hotel leak?

"We can't divulge details about the crime, Ms. Willie, as you know. What I can tell you is that a murder was committed, and a life was taken. We are asking anyone with information about this crime to call the Virginia Beach Second Precinct at 555-2300."

"We understand she was a Russian doing part-time work as a maid, and that she worked for Nikolai Ivanov. Is that correct?"

"We can't discuss details of the case at this time. Now, I have a crime to solve, Ms. Willie. Thank you."

8

June 23, 12:04 p.m.

The Poseidon, 2ⁿᵈ floor executive suite

Virginia Beach

VERA GUSAROV'S FACE WAS A MESS. Her eyes were puffy, snot was hanging from her nose and tears had carried mascara down her cheeks and onto the table. She was 22, according to her papers and—in spite of her present state—it was obvious to Ordberg, Jameson and Paige that she was a very attractive young woman.

She sat on one side of the conference table with Michelle; Rick and Ordberg sat across from her. They had already expressed their condolences, and she now stared across the table, anxiously waiting for the lieutenant to start the interview.

"Tell us about your relationship with the victim, Natasha Lischininsky," he began.

She looked down and sniffled, then composed herself.

"We meet last year at Mr. Ivanov's party. She was nice."

"What was the party for?"

"For workers of company, the Tsarina."

"Were there any male employees at this party?"

"What? I don't understand."

"Boys. Were there any boys who worked for Mr. Ivanov?"

She paused, looking down again. "Yes, maybe."

Ordberg paused and looked over at Rick.

"What is your job with Ivanov?" asked Rick.

"Maid," she replied, looking him in the eyes. "Just maid."

"Were you working as a maid at the party?"

Her head jerked back with a start and shot a look of defiance. "Nyet. I was free woman that night."

"But you really aren't free at night, are you, Vera? Look at you, you're beautiful. Men would pay a lot of money to spend special time with you, right? What do you get, $500 a night?"

She began crying again, and buried her head in her crossed arms. Michelle patted her shoulder, reassuring her that everything was going to be okay.

"We're not here to arrest you, Vera," said Ordberg. "We aren't going to take away your green card, though we could. We know all about what you and some of Ivanov's girls do at night."

Vera suddenly shot up out of her chair, her arms thrust in front of her.

"You not tell Ivanov! He kill me." She looked down at Michelle, who took her arm and guided her back into the chair, speaking gently to calm her down.

"We won't say anything to Ivanov or anyone else, Vera," said Michelle. "You can trust us." She pointed over to Ordberg and Rick. "They are the good guys. They want to help find who killed your friend."

Vera pointed to Rick and said, "This one, he like you, yes? He look okay. Maybe not like pretty boy next one, but he good."

Rick and Ordberg both laughed. Vera smiled shyly, and the tension broke.

"So what's it like being a maid at a nice hotel like the Poseidon?" asked Rick with an easy smile, which Vera returned.

"Is hard work, but good work. Sometimes good tips leave by guest."

"Where did Natasha work?" asked Ordberg, suddenly shifting gears.

"First she was work at Ramada on 5th Street."

"First?"

"Da. She start work with Mr. Ivanov maybe two month back."

Ordberg's phone buzzed, and he checked it. "Tonya has something to show us," he said, standing. "Perhaps we will go and take a look." Rick and Michelle stood.

"Vera," he said to the still-seated woman. "A policeman is going to finish the interview, and we may want to talk to you again. Please don't leave the city."

"Can I keep work?"

"By all means, just don't leave town. If you leave or do anything wrong, you will be sent back to Russia. I don't want that to happen to you." He walked around the table and handed her a card. "Call me if you think of anything, Vera. Anything at all."

He spoke briefly with a uniformed officer, motioned the

others to follow him, and headed out to find Tonya.

Sergei watched Ordberg walk across the lobby and smiled. He had hoped it would be the "Dapper Detective" as he had been called in the paper, the cop who seemed to solve the tough cases in record time. He did look good. Too bad he had to travel with that idiot surfer PI and his psychic bitch. Now that he saw her up close, he thought she looked promising, and enjoyed the way her body moved. She reminded him of his first love, the woman who broke his heart back in the early days, before he became an artist.

Perhaps she would make a great piece of art to go with her great piece of ass, he thought, and his smile widened.

9

June 23, 12:44 p.m.
Poseidon security center
Virginia Beach

THEY FOUND TONYA AND MICK sitting at a computer in the Poseidon security center on the first floor, with four 27" LED monitors wrapped around them. The room was dimly lit and cooled to offset the heat output of the racks of servers, monitors and other equipment. One armed security officer guarded the room, and three "agents" worked at various computers situated in neat rows.

On the main wall were 40 12" color monitors with live feeds from the video cameras located around the hotel. The lobby alone had six. Each could be independently operated, zoomed and panned by anyone in the security center. Next to the monitors was a 60" display showing a map of the hotel, and the location of each employee. This was made possible by attaching a GPS transponder to the name badge of every employee.

Tonya made the introductions. "Loo, this is Brad Williams, security chief here at the hotel. Brad, this is my boss, Lieutenant Ordberg." They shook hands and sized each other up.

"I do believe," began Ordberg, putting his hands out to indicate Williams, "that Mr. Zanella would be the boss today, unless I'm mistaken about your suit."

"It is indeed a Zanella, Lieutenant," replied Williams with a smile, unbuttoning his jacket and shooting his cuffs. "You know your suits. I have to say, this one is a treat to wear, very light and easy and—most important—on sale at Beecroft." They shared a laugh.

"Excellent, I shall talk to Craig."

Rick cut in between the men and shook William's hand.

"Rick Jameson. Now if you girls are finished with the runway stuff, I'd like to see what Tonya has for us." They turned to Tonya, who pulled up an image on the big screen, and turned with a flourish.

"Gentlemen, and lady, I present to you, suspect número uno. This is a video grab of a Mr. Stefan Magritte, who rented room 2013 with a credit card three days ago, in the name of—you guessed it—Stefan Magritte." She hit a few keys and brought up a second image. "Here he is getting off the 20th floor elevator and then," a new image appeared, "here he is entering his room. Both of these images were captured at approximately 12:30 a.m. today."

"But wait, there's more," she said, pulling up another three images. "Here is our victim, entering the hotel lobby at 2:35 a.m., getting off the elevator and knocking on his door. Okay hang on." She tapped the forward arrow and the frames jumped forward until a man stepped out of the door, kissed the woman's hand and led her inside.

"Finally, here's the perp leaving the scene at 4:15 a.m. this morning. Loo, we got this guy nailed to the post."

"So it would seem, Tonya," replied Ordberg, "so it would seem. And let me guess, we have an address for Mr. Magritte?"

Tonya smiled as she handed Ordberg a sheet. He read the address and looked up with a frown.

"But this is local. Are you sure about this?"

"Absolutely, sir. Magritte is a Canadian importer, mostly of alcoholic beverages and wood products. He has a house here at the Beach, and also lives in Montreal."

"Did you get his DMV photo?"

"I thought you'd never ask, Loo." She pulled up two side-by-side images. He was about 50; fairly good-looking and in good shape, with medium-length brown hair, clean shaven and no glasses. The photos appeared to be of the same man.

"So let me get this straight," said Rick, looking at the photos. "This guy has a house within a mile from here, yet he rents the most expensive suite at the most expensive hotel using his own credit card, then he hires a girl for sex and kills her. And then what? He goes back home?"

"It doesn't feel right," said Michelle. "Our guy is methodical and clean, precise and careful. Leaving a trail back to his house just doesn't fit."

"Sometimes, Michelle," replied Ordberg, "guys just want to get caught. Maybe we got lucky with this one. But lucky or not, we're gonna take him down. Let's get back to the Precinct, get a warrant and get tactical."

10

June 23, 4:35 p.m.

312 Arctic Crescent, Magritte's residence

Virginia Beach

ORDBERG, JACKSON AND JAMESON waited inside a white SWAT van parked four houses down from the suspect's. They each wore kevlar vests and windbreakers with POLICE written in five-inch letters. The Ford Econoline van was equipped with video cameras and other sensors hidden in the sign on top of the van masquerading as A-Plus Plumbing.

It could hold ten people in jump seats, as well as racks of weapons, night-vision goggles, vests and other tactical gear used on busts and similar raids. A technician monitored the sound output from a special long-distance mic that could pick up sounds through walls.

"What have you got, Bobby?" Ordberg asked the technician, who was listening intently with both hands over his headset. He twisted a knob on his display, listened for another ten seconds, then pulled off the headphones and turned to the lieutenant.

"We definitely have at least one person in the house, Loo. Could be two people, but I think this guy's alone. Sounds like he's listening to a hockey game while running on a treadmill. Don't quote me on that, but that's what it sounds like."

Ordberg patted Bobby on the back and turned to Sergeant Willard, the SWAT team leader. "Willy, I don't see any need for diversion or a pizza delivery here. I say we go in obvious and go in hard. What do you think?"

"I agree, Loo," said Willard, "Especially now that he's making a lot of noise, it's the perfect cover for us to go in hot. Let's ram the door and take this guy down."

Willard turned to Joe the "Hammer", so named due to the large hammer he carried. "Hammer, you climb that little deck out back and double click when you're in position. Capisce? Good. Okay Loo, we're ready."

Ordberg looked at the team and held up a search warrant. "Gentlemen and lady," he said with a nod to Paige, "our perp killed a young woman this morning by slicing her throat down to the bone and painting a scene with her blood. We have him cold and we have a warrant. I want this to go down clean and I want him alive if at all possible. No shooting unless he has or goes for a weapon. Is that clear?"

A chorus of "yessirs" and head nods, and Ordberg turned to Willard saying, "Your show, Willy."

"Lock and load, people," Willard said, and nine weapons were made ready, the sounds of slides and pump actions filling the van. He pressed a mic key on his vest and said, "Team 2, go go go!"

Team 2 was led by two of the biggest members who, in addition to weapons, carried a 90-pound door sledge. They double-timed their way up the street, through the yard, and up the stairs of the target house.

The rest of the team waited on the lower steps as the sledge team prepared to break open the door on Willard's signal. He had a hand over his earpiece and—after getting the double-click from Joe, now positioned at the back door—he pointed at the sledge and said, "Take it down."

The door exploded inward as the sledge took it and part of the frame with it. The handlers broke left and right, grabbing their weapons. Willard followed, bellowing "POLICE, POLICE, POLICE," as he ran straight into the room. Simultaneous to the door busting, the glass door in the back was taken out by Joe's hammer. It took him three swings to clear a space and enter the house, weapon drawn.

Within four seconds, ten weapons were leveled on the suspect, who stood, gape-mouthed, sweating on a treadmill, where he had in fact been watching a hockey game on a large LCD display. He appeared to be completely terrorized and made no move of protest, nor did he have a weapon. He was quickly cuffed and held by Joe.

Ordberg approached the terrified suspect and said, "Mr. Magritte, my name is Lieutenant Ordberg. You are under arrest for the murder of Natasha Lischininsky. You have the right to remain silent."

Ordberg led Magritte carefully through the front door. "Anything you say can and will be used against you in a court of law."

He held his arm tightly as they navigated the stairs, for Magritte's hands were cuffed behind him, and he was still in a state of shock. "You have a right to an attorney. If you cannot afford an attorney, one will be appointed for you. Do you understand these rights I just read you?"

As they approached a police cruiser with two waiting officers, Magritte finally spoke. "I want an attorney."

Sergei had watched the scene unfold from inside his heavily tinted GT, several houses down the street. He laughed out loud when he saw the SWAT team start running. "Get him, boys!" he yelled. And then within ten minutes he saw the terrified Mr. Magritte being led in cuffs out of his house and into a police cruiser. "So sorry, Magritte, but I really needed you for a bit." As he drove slowly away, Sergei felt the hunting urge rise in him again and was seized by the desire to paint another masterpiece. He could smell the paint and the blood and see the various pieces of his new tableau come together in his mind, and he anticipated the sexual release his new creation would give him. He lusted.

11

June 23, 7:10 p.m.

Second Precinct, interrogation room 2

Virginia Beach

MICHELLE PAIGE WATCHED and listened along with Tonya Jackson, Rick Jameson and Commonwealth Attorney Barbara Allen. They stood behind a large one-way glass panel, beyond which Magritte waited, hands freed, with his attorney, Roger Roman, one of the better known defense attorneys from Wilcox & Savage, a prestigious law firm in the area.

"This guy's a big swingin' dick," offered Rick, "to pull Roman down here in two hours. This is definitely gonna..."

"Shhh!" said Allen, grabbing his arm. "I don't want to miss this."

Ordberg entered the interrogation room, introduced himself and took a chair across from Magritte and Roman, who immediately launched his attack.

"This is highly outrageous! My client is a well-respected

member of society, an important businessman who brings a significant amount of tax revenue into this city. You have no right to break into his house and attack him in broad daylight. His reputation may be ruined now, thanks to you and your SWAT team!"

Ordberg calmly waited out Roman's outburst, after which he looked the attorney directly in the eye, and waited. Roman blinked first, looking down at his files, muttering to himself.

"Ordberg's smooth," said Michelle. "He just established dominance in the room without saying one word. He's good." They continued watching as the interrogation unfolded on the other side of the glass.

Finally Ordberg slid a copy of the search warrant over to Roman.

"Mr. Roman, this is a duly authorized and signed search warrant giving us the right to enter and search your client's house and arrest him." He gave Roman a chance to read the document and note the signature of Judge Bailey, a venerable jurist.

Ordberg then laid out and explained the photos that Tonya had displayed at the Poseidon; the DMV photo, the various photos from the Poseidon security cameras and the credit card receipt with Magritte's name on it. In total, it was damning evidence and Roman looked at his client for a beat, then turned back to Ordberg.

"May I have a word with my client, Lieutenant?"

"Absolutely, Mr. Roman," said Ordberg, rising from his seat. "Just give us the high sign when you're done, please," pointing to the mirror behind him.

"Oh, I'll wave alright. And remind Barbara that the sound must be turned off while I'm alone with my client. If it is not, she will have a civil complaint against VBPD and her office by close of business today. Do I make myself clear, Lieutenant?"

"Perfectly clear," he replied, walking out of the room to join the others.

"What do you think so far?" he asked Allen.

"I think," she replied, "I want to hear what they have to say. But the evidence so far is solid."

"I'm not so sure," ventured Michelle. They turned to her expectantly. "The guy we're looking at does not fit the MO, just based on his physical and emotional mannerisms. This guy is withdrawn, shy and clearly frightened. You guys said he was like Bambi during the raid, right, in a state of shock? That doesn't sound like our guy. John, I know what you said about some guys wanting to be caught, but this doesn't feel like that to me. This feels like a completely different guy."

"Could he have multiple personalities?" asked Tonya.

"Maybe," admitted Michelle. "I won't know that until I can interview him."

"Not so sure that will be possible," replied Ordberg, "Roman is on the warpath, and he can shut down access to his client if he wants."

"Okay, Loo," said Allen, pointing through the glass to a waving Roman, "Looks like you still have access. Off you go." Ordberg re-entered the room and waited for Roman to speak.

"My client wants to cooperate fully with you to clear his name and help bring the killer to justice."

"That is most excellent, Mr. Magritte," began Ordberg. He held up a color print of the DMV license photo. "Is this a photograph of you, Mr. Magritte?"

"Yes, that looks like the photo on my license. Let me give you the real thing." He pulled out his wallet, removed his license and laid it on the table. The photos matched.

Ordberg then pushed forward the credit card receipt for the Poseidon suite. "Is this your credit card number?"

"Yes, I think so." He pulled out his card from his wallet and laid that beside his license. The numbers matched. "But I never bought that room. Someone must have stolen my number."

"Stealing your credit card number is relatively easy," replied Ordberg, "but the problem is getting your 3-number security code. Much more difficult, but not impossible." He slid forward the screen shots from the security cameras. "Is this you, Mr. Magritte?"

Magritte studied the photos. "It would appear to be me, no question. But it must be an imposter!" He turned to his attorney and threw up both hands. "Why would anyone want to be me?"

"Are you suggesting that the murderer assumed your complete identity, physical and digital, and so portrayed himself to avoid detection?"

"Oui."

"Mr. Magritte, according to the evidence laid before you, at approximately 3:00 a.m. today, you murdered a young woman in cold blood at the Poseidon. Do you deny this?"

"What time did you say the murder occurred?"

"Sometime between two and three o'clock this morning."

"Fantastik! Then I could not have done it!"

"Why do you say that, Mr. Magritte?"

"Because I was in the emergency room of the Beach hospital for most of the night. I'm sure they can verify this."

"Why were you there?"

"I thought I was having a heart attack. But thank God it was just gas!"

12

June 24, 6:30 a.m.

61st Street beach

Virginia Beach

THEY HAD ALREADY WATCHED the sun come up over the ocean against a cloudless sky. Now they were surfing head-high waves near the temporary pier the city had built to install a new $30 million storm water system. It was an absolute eyesore, but a surfer's delight because piers create sandbars, sandbars create breaks, and breaks are great friends to all surfers.

"Holy shit!" yelled Mick Gorbach, as he and Rick Jameson duck-dived their long boards under a mountainous wave. They had just ridden a huge, clean wave in, and were paddling back out for more. "This can't be Virginia Beach. This is more like Hatteras. Head-high and clean *here*? Are we dreamin', bro?"

"It's a good dream, Mick. A very good dream." They positioned themselves just past the break and sat on their boards, doing what surfers do: stare out at the ocean and watch for the telltale signs of a good set, daydream, and tell stories about surfing and life. Rick had always thought that if Michelle could do her therapy sessions on surfboards, all her clients would be cured in no time.

Surfing reminded him of hunting and fishing, two other pastimes he enjoyed— the great pleasure and planning involved in making a good shot, landing a big fish, and now, catching the perfect wave. But aside from the thrill of the kill and riding that wave, just being out there on a boat, in a duck blind or now, just sitting on his board with a friend to share in the experience was the only therapy he needed or hoped to ever have in his life.

"I figure I'll be out here at least into my 70s."

Mick laughed. "So you got what, ten years?"

"Bite me!" Rick caught a wave and shot the still laughing Mick the bird, shouting, "Learn from your elders, punk!" Mick enjoyed his boss's lesson and thrilled to the ride from his seat on his board. Rick walked up to the nose of his board and did a classic "hang ten," then lifted one foot up into the *Karate Kid* stance with his arms straight out. He performed the kick perfectly, but landed awkwardly and fell off his board, which shot high into the air and dragged him by his leash, caught in the violence of the wave.

As Rick recovered his board and paddled back out to join Mick, he thought again about the case of the Russian maid. He and Mick and their firm had plenty of other work to keep him busy, and he loved the work he did for his clients. But truth be told, working on a murder case really made his juices flow and brought back all the memories from his job as a NYPD detective, back in the day.

He knew that the killer in this case was flipping them

all the bird with the sheer audacity of his crime: meticulous planning, attention to detail, chutzpah, and gruesome delivery. This was an adversary worthy of respect, along with a couple of bullets, the first in his crotch. Ouch, sorry about that, meant to shoot you in the heart, you crazy fuck!

He pulled up next to Mick and they watched the swells for a while, in no hurry.

"So what do you think about the bad guy, Boss?" asked Mick. "Why'd he off that chick?"

"He's educated and smart. They can be mutually exclusive, but this guy has both. He's got plenty of money and understands how to use it. Not spend it, but *use* it to get his way. He's a visionary guy and most definitely a sick murdering mastermind. We probably know him already."

"I agree with all that, but why'd he do it?"

"I don't know, Mick. Not yet. I do know he's making some kind of a statement. He wants to be seen but not caught. He's staging everything."

"You mean like in a movie?"

"Yeah, exactly like in a movie. He went to the trouble of getting a fake ID of a local guy and then becoming that guy so we'd take the bait and go down that rabbit hole and arrest the wrong man. How much you want to bet he was at the scene when we took down Magritte?"

"No shit?"

"No shit. Michelle's working on a profile, so some of this is coming out of that. She's not sure yet if this dude's a sociopath. Plenty of signs saying he is, but some saying he ain't."

"If he's a sociopath it means he doesn't care about people."

"Yes, but it's more complicated than that. He may in fact have cared deeply about that Russian chick he killed. Just not in the normal way we think. The big difference is in the whole 'sanctity of life' thing. We think about murder and hurting others for personal gain as absolutely wrong. It's reflexive, instinctive. But a sociopath thinks only in terms of what is good for him. He thinks about people like he thinks about money or cars or things: they are there for his benefit and he has the right to use them any way he chooses."

"We need to catch this guy, Rick. Personally, I'd like to kick the shit out of him."

"Me too, brother-man. Me too. In the meantime, see if you can catch this wave, little boy!"

Rick was fast but Mick faster as they paddled and launched themselves down the face of the wave. It broke cleanly to the north, pushing them toward the pier. Rick turned out of the wave and paddled back out, while Mick stayed on the wave to "shoot" the pier.

Rick laughed as Mick whooped with joy, his middle finger saluting the air, riding the wave all the way down to 63rd Street.

13

June 25, 7:30 a.m.

Wareing's Gym

Virginia Beach

TONYA AND RICK HAD BEEN sparring more than five minutes, and both were drenched with sweat. Each wore tight shorts, ankle/calf protectors, t-shirts, lightweight kick-boxing gloves and protective headgear.

A crowd had formed to watch the well-known pair whirl around the ring in a fast-moving choreography of fluid form. During this phase of their warm-up, they did not attempt to connect with their kicks and punches. Instead, they worked on body alignment and footwork, sometimes stopping to offer advice to each other about a particular move.

Now they were ready to fight. They walked to opposite sides of the ring and bowed to each other, touched gloves, then assumed classic Taekwondo stances. They began to circle each other, jabbing with their gloves, feeling the distance. Tonya was the aggressor—by design—and the crowd loved it.

"Get him, Tonya!" several women in the crowd shouted. Suddenly Tonya feinted left and turned quickly to unleash a side kick at Rick's belly, but Rick was already moving back, grabbed her leg and pulled it up, lifting her completely off the ground. Tonya turned in midair and landed on her hands, somersaulting quickly back onto her feet again. The crowd applauded her recovery.

"So Magritte walks," began Tonya, as she circled her opponent. "Dude's got an alibi made in heaven. Which means our guy is a master of disguise, right?"

"Yeah," replied Rick as he threw a combination punch that rocked Tonya back on her heels. "We had a guy in Queens once who worked in movies. Had a complete makeup kit, wardrobe, you name it."

"How'd you catch him?"

"He found us. One of our dicks was interviewing the manager of a costume shop when in walks the bad guy." He blocked a quick succession of punches and completely missed Tonya's step-over kick, which took him hard on his left thigh, forcing him to step back. The crowd cheered.

Rick quit talking and concentrated on his technique. They fell back into a rhythm of fighting they both enjoyed. Box, spin, kick, punch: an endless variation of motion, power and grace.

"So what happened to the guy?" asked Tonya.

"He made the mistake of rabbiting from the shop, got caught, and now the state feeds him three squares a day, free of charge, throw away the lock and key. If the dude hadn't run, our guy might not have spotted him. He was—after all—a master of disguise, and we didn't really know what he looked like."

"So now what?"

"Now we do what we did up north. We start backtracking and following leads. You want to be a detective, right?"

"You know I do, Rick!" This said with a flurry of punches.

Rick laughed, easily fending off and blocking the punches. Tonya was strong but—more importantly—she was fast, and while Rick was stronger and more experienced, he had to use all of his skills to stay ahead of her. Still, he knew her weakness, the best way to get her to lose her focus.

"Hey, Ton, shouldn't you be checking on your boys about now?" When she paused to consider his question, her guard lowered a touch, and he executed a perfect low sidekick, sweeping her legs out from under her. She landed hard on her ass. But as luck would have it—not to mention the bounce afforded by the boxing ring—she was able to bounce straight back up into a standing position, much to the delight of the ladies in the crowd.

"You gotta keep your focus, Tonya. Can't let anything get in the way when the shit goes down. I'm only doing this for your own good, kid, you know that, right?" He stopped fighting and put out his glove. "Friends?"

Tonya raised her glove to tap his, but at the last minute lunged under and cross-punched him in the chest with every bit of her 122 pounds. As Rick careened backwards, his arms wind-milling to recover his balance, Tonya swept out his feet and followed his body down onto the mat, where he landed on his back with a thunderous noise.

To the sound of cheering and applause, Tonya straddled her slightly pissed—and completely surprised—sparring partner and said, "You gotta keep your focus, Rick. I'm only doing this for your own good. You know that, right?"

14

June 30, 12:46 a.m.

Fort Story, American Indian village

Virginia Beach

"POP!"

They both exploded with laughter as the cork violently erupted from their second bottle of Cristal; "only the best" was Sergei's favorite expression. It hit nothing but sky on the top-down black convertible Mustang GT Cobra, shooting up like a rocket twenty feet above them, then returning to bounce off the dashboard, landing on the seat precisely below Sergei's crotch. He looked over at his date, his latest art project, with a raised eyebrow. The both laughed again.

Her name was Victoria, a tall Russian brunette with green eyes and the body of a goddess. Sergei had loved every minute he spent with her over the past month, building their relationship and earning her trust. Part of him wished it could go on forever but he knew that could never be, for the show must go on. All that mattered was his art. He knew this could be accomplished only by the creation of another masterpiece, and nothing was going to stop him, especially not trivial romance.

At first it was purely a business relationship: she gave him sex and in return he gave her money—quite a lot of it. After a while his charm—and his money—won her favor to the point she freely gave herself to him. He was handsome and single, a successful American businessman who freely lavished her with gifts, and she was beginning to think he could be the rich American husband she dreamed would make all her dreams come true.

Victoria reached down to his crotch, brushing his manhood lightly with her fingers, and grabbed the cork. She held it up and sniffed it, saying, "I keep this for later, remind me of Sergei Rocket Man!"

She watched as Sergei got out of the car and came around to open her door, ever the gentleman, and once again dreamed of a new life, the life that eluded her so far. She wanted more than anything to live in this prosperous country, and she hoped that Sergei would be the one to free her once and for all from the poverty-stricken ghetto in Russia where her family lived and died.

After all, she thought, his name was Russian, so it must be a sign from heaven. She lit candles and special blessed incense she had purchased from the Heritage Store. The aroma and smoke danced beneath the beautiful golden cross her mother had given her two years ago, just before she boarded the plane for America. It was not just any cross, but the Golgotha family cross, handed down over the centuries and blessed by many priests and holy men. It was given to Victoria in the hope that she would become rich and save the family. She prayed for that to come to pass, and hoped that God would hear her prayers and release her from the life of sin she was living. Please God!

She was exuberant tonight; excited about their crazy nighttime excursion into the darkness and her chance to perform on a real stage. That had been a dream of hers since she was a young girl– to become a woman of the arts. Tonight she would become the actress she always dreamed she might be.

They were parked on 89th Street, close to the entrance to Fort Story, with easy beach access for a little "black ops" as Sergei put it. He walked around the front of the Mustang, looking down at the chrome snake decal on the hood and admiring it. He loved his life, his art, his genius, and tonight he would love this woman—and make her last forever.

After gallantly helping her out of the car and stabilizing her while she removed her red Jimmy Choo stilettos, he handed her a strap-on headlamp and said, "Your mission, Victoria, should you choose to accept it, is to follow me and do whatever I tell you." She laughed and followed him down the dark street, up and over the dunes and out to the beach.

They walked north for a few hundred yards, and then Sergei led them back over the dunes, using a boardwalk recently built from synthetic boards. As he helped Victoria up onto the boardwalk, she asked, "What is this, Sergei? I get splinters!"

"No splinters, my love. This is a special runway that will carry us across the sands and launch you into stardom. You shall become timeless beside the waves. An ocean star! Timeless as Marilyn Monroe."

"Marilyn Monroe? I know this woman, she very beautiful. Sergei you make me laugh. This runway look new. Did you make it for me, Sergei dear?"

"Yes I did, Victoria, just for you. Tonight I made everything new, just for you!"

"Will you really make me American princess?"

"Oh yes, my love. Tonight all your dreams will come true."

Sergei took her hand and led her over the dunes and onto a sandy road. Soon a row of bleachers came into view, then a round wooden stage. This was the outdoor theater for *1607: First Landing*, a play that ran each summer telling the story of local Indians and the colonists who landed here in the early 1600s.

Sergei hurled his backpack up onto the raised stage and walked underneath to an area that housed various dressing rooms and supplies for the play. He removed his trusty Leatherman and inserted the screwdriver into the latch on the door marked "Wardrobe." Within moments the door was open and he turned on the lights.

"You are burglar, too!" laughed Victoria.

Sergei had already scouted the location, so it took no time to assemble the outfits and props for his own modern-day version of *1607*. Victoria followed him up the stairs and onto the large round stage. It was a beautiful, cloudless night, and the new moon cast a sliver of light onto the deserted, eerie stage. Victoria walked around, curtsying to the invisible audience and blowing them kisses. "Thank you so much," she said. "I love you, too."

Sergei laid out the wardrobe and the travel-sized makeup kit he had brought. She was so beautiful, he thought, and paused to watch her. She was a natural performer and he guessed she would have done well on the stage. Tonight would be her final performance though—her curtain call—and he was touched with a momentary pang of regret. But the feeling passed quickly, as he embraced the passionate thrill of what lay ahead. He had become The Director.

"Come, my darling Victoria," he said, holding up the

Indian princess dress, richly adorned with sequins, beads and bits of oyster shell woven into the chest piece and fringe. She turned and walked slowly toward him, vamping in a sexy version of a runway model. Then she stopped and slowly, teasingly stripped until she stood naked before him, her hands lightly playing across her breasts, belly and pudendum.

"Come, Mr. Big Chief Sergei. I need hot Indian love."

Sergei was completely mesmerized by the sight of her, and his lust burst into a fire of desire. He longed to take her right then, but he shook his head and said, "After, my love, after the show. First you perform for me, then you get heap big Indian love."

She smiled, turned and put her arms up, and he dropped the dress onto her body; it was a perfect fit. She twirled and danced around, causing the tassels and leather thongs to fly out in a pretty arc. She danced to her own internal music, already assuming the role of the Indian princess.

"Dance with me, Sergei," she demanded.

"Not here, my love, you must dance with The Seven Princesses."

She clapped her hands together. "Good, where are these princesses?"

He grabbed his bag and led her down off the stage and away from the beach, back toward the Indian village. They walked through a low scrub forest. Each tree had been windswept and trained by the northeasterly ocean winds and they all leaned toward the southwest, like chanting monks with outstretched arms. Soon they were surrounded by strange, low, rounded buildings: an Indian village created for school tours as part of the historic site. Sergei led them through a low door into a vaulted hut made of sticks and reed mats.

"Those spooky," she said, after Sergei bumped into two

hanging mobiles. "What they are?"

"What are they?" Sergei corrected her. "They're dream catchers. The Indians—the people who lived here before white people came—say they catch dreams and protect them."

"Good. I give them my dreams."

"What do you dream of?" He took her into his arms, smiling.

"My dreams private," she whispered into his ear and pushed him away with a laugh. Then she pointed at the dream catcher and asked, "Do they really catch bad dreams?"

Sergei motioned her closer, shining his headlamp on the dream catcher. "Can you see how the wooden vines are woven together to form this circle? The circle represents the circle of life, and the web work is there to catch all the bad dreams."

"Yes, Sergei, I see how it works!"

"The web would catch and hold the bad dreams until the sun rose the next day, and the light of dawn would strike them, destroying them forever."

"I want one!" She tugged his hand toward the door. "This place spooky. Come, Big Chief, where are Indian Princesses?"

He led her away from the hut to an open, circular clearing surrounded by the village buildings. In the middle of the clearing were seven wooden poles placed in a perfect circle, each pole 12 feet high; faces had been carved on each. The moonlight cast spooky shadows on the site, yet it was also entrancing and beautiful.

Victoria clapped her hands again and ran into the circle. She curtsied to each pole, saying, "So good to meet you, Princess. I am Princess Victoria!" She examined one of the poles, saying, "Sergei, what is written on pole?"

He read, "Princess Natima." Victoria clapped her hands

again as Sergei walked back to the middle of the clearing.

"These are the Seven Princesses," he said. "You must kneel before them and ask permission to become a princess with them, Victoria. You will become Princess Eight. Come here into the center, where I've prepared a place for you."

"Princess Eight! I love it." She ran to him and kneeled, facing one of the poles.

Sergei stood behind her, stroking her hair. "Yes, tonight Princess Eight will become an immortal actress, never forgotten. Tonight we will make art under the moonlight."

Victoria closed her eyes, folded her hands and prayed to her God to make it so, just as Sergei had said. She promised to be good and to quit making bad choices. Please God, she prayed, let me marry Sergei and start my new life here. Let me save my family.

As she prayed, Sergei pulled out and unfolded an antique 6-inch straight razor. It was beautifully inlaid, a work of art, and extremely sharp. He smiled as she prayed and brought the razor down to close Victoria's final performance.

15

June 30, 5:23 a.m.

Fort Story, 1607 stage

Virginia Beach

THE DAWN SKY CAST A PASTEL light onto the grassy area of the killer's new set. Ordberg, Jameson, Paige and Jackson, along with Captain Rogers and Chief Willie, were in a huddle around the body.

"Holy shit!" said Rogers, "we got us a real live serial killer." He turned to the chief and asked, "What did the Mayor say?"

"What do you think he said?" Chief Willie said with irritation. "He sure as shit didn't ask how my portfolio was doing." He looked around the group. "People, we are in deep shit here, and our asses are on the line. Hansen and the rest of the big hotel owners are going nuts, worried about bookings. When the word gets out that we have a serial killer on the loose, they will most assuredly lose money. And when the hotels lose money, the mayor gets a ration of shit, which travels downhill to me and now... to you." The last was said while poking the chest of Captain Rogers.

He turned to Ordberg. "Lieutenant, you're running this case. I've authorized access to whatever you need. Please tell me you've got something good for me."

Ordberg, well dressed as ever in a blue blazer, polo shirt and khakis with loafers, quickly consulted his iPhone while multiple flashes lit the area as the technicians began recording the scene. More vehicles were arriving.

"Her name's Victoria Kirelen, Chief. Her ID was on her, along with her passport. We ran her file: she's on an extended work visa, employed by Tsarina Enterprises..."

"Well, of course she is," blurted Jameson. The Chief turned on him, his face reddening.

"You got a problem, Jameson? Ivanov is a friend of the mayor, and one of the city's biggest employers. Two of his employees just got murdered, and my people are here, playing in the sand at the beach. Why are you even on this case?"

Captain Rogers took a step forward, interjecting, "Chief, you'll have to forgive Rick. We've been investigating Tsarina for a while, and it would appear they have a thriving night business in addition to their legitimate employment company. We're meeting with him later today, sir, and will discuss the murders and his company's possible involvement with prostitution."

The Chief stared at Jameson for a few beats, then turned to Rogers. "Okay, Len, what else you got?"

Ordberg continued. "Kirilen was employed by Tsarina for the past two years. First as a maid, then as an administrative assistant in the executive offices, and as a part-time model at Maxima Boutique, which is owned by..."

"Brandy West," finished the Chief. "So what's her

connection to all this?"

"She's dating Ivanov and we suspect she may be running his escort service."

"No shit? Are you telling me Brandy West may be a madam? Seriously, do you guys know who she's connected to?"

"Yes sir, we suspect she is Ivanov's madam and may be providing escorts to some local heavy hitters."

"Let's tread carefully here, people. Check out Ivanov, but concentrate on the murder. I don't want a second investigation screwing things up. We got enough heat as it is, and I don't want you guys busting open another hornet's nest. Is that clear, Captain?"

"Yes sir, perfectly clear. We'll concentrate on the murders."

"Great," he said, turning back to Ordberg. "Give me the rest, Loo."

Ordberg glanced at his iPhone again. "Kirilen was a beautiful woman, as you can see. She was 23, same age as the previous vic. They entered the site from the beach, broke into the wardrobe and prop closet under the stage and took the items she's wearing and the rest of the props out here." The Chief turned to look at the body again.

The victim was naked, face up, with her arms and legs splayed out in a perfect X, each limb tied to what appeared to be tent stakes. As with the previous victim, her neck had been brutally cut down to the bone and her blood had sprayed around her like an aura. Enormous ocher-colored wings were traced in the sand, sprouting from her arms and extending eight feet out from her body. When viewed from her feet, she appeared to be flying.

"What's that thing around her neck?" asked the Chief.

"It's called a dream catcher, chief," replied Ordberg.

"Native American spiritual heritage. The curator said it was taken from one of the lodges in the Indian village."

"Well, damn," said the Chief, turning to Michelle Paige. "Next they'll be pulling tarot cards out of her ass, right Paige?"

"I wouldn't be surprised, sir," Paige deadpanned, "But it wouldn't quite fit the scene he's created here. The wings look like they came from a Renaissance angel. They really are quite beautifully rendered, considering the medium. And her hair and makeup were done with much more care than the last victim, which seems crude by comparison to this one. This all makes me think he was fond of the victim. I didn't get that from the last one, but I feel like this was arranged with love."

"Are you shittin' me?" asked Captain Rogers. "Since when does a guy express his love for a girl by cutting her head halfway off her neck, spraying her blood around after he offs her. Seems more like hate to me, Michelle. Hatred from a sicko."

"I agree he's sick, sir. But I get the feeling that he knew this girl. He cared for her. Even the way he tied her down is different, like he didn't want to hurt her."

"Oh, he hurt her," said Rogers, shaking his head as he looked down at the body, "He hurt her plenty."

"So what's the plan, Loo?" interrupted the Chief, turning to Ordberg.

"We've got teams working on the theatre and acting angles and we're also running the Russian connection through the feds. Forensics is still working on the evidence: wig fibers, the stakes, line, makeup, you name it, we're running it down. But so far, no hits, which just adds to the M.O. of a meticulous perp. We're checking with local military for any guys who were booted for sexual stuff. And we're meeting Monday with Ivanov."

"Okay, Loo, sounds good. Just remember that our favorite Russian's got friends in high places. If he's involved, take his ass down. Otherwise, be careful. And keep me posted, Len."

He turned to leave, then turned back in a perfect imitation of Columbo. "One more thing. The Mayor made some calls. We're pulling in some outside talent from the Fibs. That's the FBI, Michelle," he said with sarcasm. "So that's the bad news. The good news is the Fibs sent us a Russian, and she's going to the Ivanov meet with you guys. Oh, Rick, even better news," he said with a smirk, "She's a looker, just your type!"

With that, he turned and quickly left, his assigned uniform cop trailing behind like a puppy.

16

July 2, 10:15 a.m.

Tsarina Enterprises

Town Center

Virginia Beach

THEY MET ELENA GRIGOREVNA at the Second Precinct and briefed her on the case, then rode together to Ivanov's office in Town Center, Virginia Beach's attempt at creating a "downtown" amidst the suburban sprawl. Grigorevna was a striking blond in her mid-thirties, the daughter of Russian diplomats who later became naturalized U.S. citizens. She had a small scar just below her bottom lip that only heightened her appeal. Fluent in English, Russian, Arabic and French, she worked in the FBI's Joint Terrorism Task Force.

She, Ordberg and Jameson entered the lush lobby of the office, where Ordberg flashed his badge and announced himself.

"Mr. Ivanov is expecting you, Lieutenant," said the

stunning young woman behind the counter with a slight accent. "Please be seated and someone will be with you shortly."

The "someone" turned out to be two large men in suits. Without ceremony, the larger of the two announced, "Mr. Ivanov will see you now. But you leave weapons here." He held out his hand expectantly.

Ordberg and Jameson laughed, and the Lieutenant started to reply when Elena put a hand on his arm and stepped forward, holding out her FBI badge. She spoke quietly and rapidly in Russian, and the two tough guys visibly wilted.

After a pause, she said quietly in English, "Do you understand?"

"Da," they replied in unison.

"Khahrohshy. Now take us to your boss and keep your mouths shut."

They did just that, and Rick and Ordberg shared a look of surprise as they entered Ivanov's large corner office.

"She's good," Rick murmured.

Nikolai Ivanov greeted them with boyish charm, escorting them to a seating area with a low mahogany table being set by a young, dark-haired beauty in a French maid's outfit.

Ivanov looked to be about 50, with streaks of silver shot through his hair. He was known as a ladies' man. Since arriving from Russia 21 years ago, shortly after the fall of the Soviet Empire, he had grown his enterprise into a Fortune 1,000 company.

He had served in the Soviet GRU, military intelligence, where he had learned English and the art of subterfuge. He was very well connected politically and liberally donated to certain campaigns. He was allegedly involved with the Russian mob, which specialized in high-ticket prostitution and other white-collar crime. But he was wiley, had clever and pricey legal fire, and had managed to avoid any charge brought against him over the years.

"Please," he said, indicating the ornate silver glassware, "It is a custom in Russia to share tea with friends. And sometimes," he said with a smile at Ordberg, "even with enemies."

He turned to his henchmen and spoke rapidly in Russian, after which they left.

"Please forgive my employees. They are very useful to me for security, but I'm afraid they are lacking in, how do you say, the social graces?" He took a sip of his dark tea. He turned to the well-dressed man on his left. "Please allow me to introduce my attorney, Mr. Eric Hester from Williams & Moore."

"You're not a suspect, Mr. Ivanov," replied Ordberg. "At least not for these crimes. We're here to talk with you about the murders of your two employees."

"I know why you are here," said Ivanov, icily. "Mr. Hester is here as counselor and witness, and to help me decide if I will take action against the city for failing to prevent the murders of my dear employees and causing my company to lose money. Do you have any idea how much I pay the Beach in taxes every year? You could say I pay for a good part of the operations of the Virginia Beach Police Department."

He set his tea down on the table, sat back in his chair, and said, "So tell me, Lieutenant, what are you doing to protect my employees?"

"Where were you on the dates of the two murders, Mr. Ivanov?" He handed over a sheet with the dates to Hester.

The attorney removed another sheet, and handed it back to Ordberg, saying, "Here are the whereabouts and alibis of my client during the periods of time the murders were committed. We have corroborating witnesses who will attest to this in court. My client is clean, Lieutenant."

"As I said before," replied Ordberg, "Mr. Ivanov is not a suspect. But thank you for this. It makes our job that much easier to remove you from suspicion, at least for these crimes."

"What are these 'other' crimes you speak of?" asked Ivanov with rising scorn.

Hester put a hand on his arm, and gestured for his client to wait.

He turned to Ordberg and said, "Please continue with your questions, Lieutenant, but limit them to the murders. Otherwise I'm afraid I'll have no choice but to end this conversation on behalf of my client."

Ordbeg nodded and continued. "Mr. Ivanov, both of the victims worked for your company as maids or in other capacities, correct?"

"That is correct."

"And did these other capacities include operating as high-priced call girls for your clients and your 'close friends'?"

Hester again placed his hand on his client's arm in a restraining manner. Ivanov's face reddened as he stared at Ordberg, then hissed, "Vy glupyĭ kusok derma."

Ordberg and Jameson both turned to Grigorevna, who quietly said, "Vy znaete vse o glupyh kuski der ma , ublyudok." Ivanov again turned red and replied, "Predatel skaya suka!"

"In English please." said Ordberg, exasperated.

Neither Ivanov or Grigorevna replied, and then Ivanov began laughing, saying to Ordberg, "You are very clever to bring this one, Lieutenant. I like her, even if she insulted my father. She is very smart." He looked her up and down. "And so beautiful, too, just the way I like them. Why don't you come work for me, Elena darling?"

"Pochemu by tebe ne poĭti yebesh sebya!"

Ivanov laughed again. "She told me to go and have sex with myself. Oh, but I'd rather have it with you, my sweet cousin. Perhaps later?" He turned back to Ordberg and said, "I'm sorry, Lietenant, but your little FBI agent has made me forget your question."

"I asked if either of the two victims worked as call girls in addition to their documented jobs with your company."

"As you can imagine, Lieutenant, we cannot keep track of our employees' outside activities. Some of them take other part-time jobs to make the ends meet. So maybe they did work as call girls. But not for me, and if you ever insult me and my company again by asking such a question, I will personally..."

Hester rose quickly from his seat and said, "Ladies and gentlemen, this meeting is over. On behalf of my client, thank you for coming. If you have any other questions for my client, please send them to my office. Here's my card. Good day to you all."

17

July 2, 10:42 a.m.

Tsarina Enterprises

Town Center

Virginia Beach

IVANOV DRANK THE SHOT of vodka in one swift motion and slammed the glass down onto his desk. Eva, one of his favorite girls, stepped forward with an inquiring look and lifted the open bottle of Dovgan. He motioned her over and stroked her thigh up to the luxurious region between her legs. She smiled as he withdrew his fingers and licked them.

"That will be all, my beauty. Daddy will be hungry for you later."

She bent down and whispered something into his ear. He laughed, smacking her her ass as she walked away.

"I want her off the list for a while, Brandy."

Brandy West was a fortyish former model and the

statuesque owner of the Maxima Boutique, an exclusive women's clothing store catering to the local carriage trade. She also planned and produced some of the biggest parties in town, and worked with Ivanov and his cronies to take care of all the needs of the local politicos and wealthy patrons who appreciated beauty and would pay handsomely for it.

She crossed her long legs, staring at Ivanov. "Eva is one of our top producers, Nicky. You know that. We need the money she brings in."

She flinched as Ivanov slapped the desk with his open palm, yelling, "You need the money, Brandy. I don't need money, but I need her. She is off market right now."

"Whatever makes you happy, Nicky," replied a now chastened Brandy.

"Good answer." Ivanov motioned for Boris and Ivan, who had been lurking near his door, to enter.

"Yes, Boss."

"Boris, you and your boys work with Brandy on the girls' schedule for the next two weeks, until they catch this svinya ublyudok. This pig fucker," he added for Brandy's sake.

"I need ten more guys, Boss. We got too many girls, they go here, there, all the time."

Ivanov turned to Mick Gorbach and said, "Mick, can you get me some muscle to bulk up our security team?"

Mick had been working for Ivanov for the past year. He kept him appraised of police investigations, goings-on in the local Russian community, and also provided mercenaries and muscle to cover events, VIP protection at some of Hansen's hotels and, of course, protection for his girls.

Ivanov had scored a major coup when he convinced Gorbach—who spoke fluent Russian—to moonlight for him when not on duty for Jameson Investigations. What he didn't know was that this was Jameson's idea, to help Ordberg's team build a case against Tsarina.

"Yeah, Nicky, I can get the muscle, but it ain't gonna come cheap. We need guys with firearm permits, everything legal. That narrows it down quite a bit. Plus we need to train them."

"Yes, everything must be legal, above the board. Ordberg is smart, but we're smarter. I want you to dig like a good little mole so we stay clean. Money is not problem. Losing two girls make price go up!" He laughed. "They kill our girls, we make more money. I love this fucking country!"

"What about FBI bitch girl?" asked Boris.

"Follow her. Push her buttons, but keep it legal, Boris."

"With pleasure, Boss, with big pleasure," he said, slapping one giant fist into his open palm.

"Great pleasure, you idiot. Great pleasure, not big pleasure."

"I will have great big pleasure, Boss!" They both laughed.

18

July 6, 9:10 P.m.

Virginia Beach United Methodist Church

212 19th Street

Virginia Beach

THE FELLOWSHIP HALL AT THE church was buzzing. About twenty homeless, including several East Europeans, and almost as many Tidewater Literacy Council volunteers were here with them. They came twice a week for literacy lessons, basic math and reading.

George had invited Tonya to observe the class, and she was impressed with the scene. George was teaching a young Latino mother with a toddler on her lap, working in the Dr. Seuss book, *Hop on Pop*.

Lo estás haciendo bien María," said George. "Vamos a intentar otra página. Maria looked adoringly at George as he high-fived her son, Hector.

"You good man," she said shyly, taking his hand. "Much

thank you."

George laughed and continued the lesson. As she watched him teach, Tonya began to compare George to her ex. He was just as charming as Ronnie had been. They both were comfortable with women, but she noticed that George had a special gift for rapport that Ronnie lacked.

Ronnie would never have had the patience to teach like this—nor would she, truth be told. He didn't really have patience even with their two boys. Having kids was tough enough, but twins added a significant amount of stress and were two primary reasons their marriage had broken apart. That and his two affairs.

George and Ronnie had been friends together in the Army, and remained so afterward. He became Uncle George to the twins and they loved spending time with him. He was a good man, an honest man, and she thanked the Lord every day for their friendship.

She knew George wanted more, but she was not ready for another relationship, even if her big bed felt so empty.

When the lesson ended, George rolled over to her and smiled. "Hey there, Ms. Tonya. Can a man buy a pretty lady a DQ ice cream?"

She looked down at him and shook her head. "You sure know how to charm a girl, George, and you know how much I love those Blizzards. But I gotta take a rain check. The meter's running on the sitter and I need to get back."

"Cool. I'll walk you to your car then."

"Walk? Who you kiddin'?"

They laughed as they crossed the street, cutting through one of the big municipal parking lots. As they approached her car a gang of five young black men sauntered over. They wore the colors, and the neck tattoos, of a Portsmouth gang that dealt in drugs and prostitution. They were trouble, and George and Tonya knew it. George quickly dialed 9-1-1 on his phone, strapped to his wheelchair seat and out of sight of the gang.

"'Sup fellas," asked George as the gang formed a semi-circle around them.

"Who you callin' 'fella,' old cripple dude?" asked the leader. He looked to be older than the others, based on the amount of gold he wore around his neck and the deference they showed him.

"We're just going to the lady's car. We don't want no trouble."

"Well, you *got* trouble, mu-fuckuh."

He walked over to Tonya and circled her. "Mmmm, mmm," he said to his boys. "This girl is tasty, ain't she?" They nodded and smiled nervously, looking around the well-lit parking lot. They were used to working the dark, down-and-out sections of Portsmouth and Norfolk, not the brightly lit parking lots of the Oceanfront.

"Skeeter, this shit is lame," said one of the larger members of the gang.

Skeeter turned to him and said, "Shut the fuck up, Jerome, you dumb nigger. Now all you all get in here. We be showin' some love to our new sister."

The first police unit to arrive, responding to George's call and the GPS triangulation of his phone location, recorded the action on their dash video camera as they approached the scene slowly, lights out.

"Skeeter?" asked George. "That's the name of a little bitty insect."

Skeeter turned away from Tonya, saying to George,

"Gonna bust you up, boy. Skeeter gonna…" He never finished the sentence. Tonya punched him so hard on the side of his head he spent six days in the hospital with a fractured skull before being transferred to the city jail. George, meanwhile, pulled a metal rod out of his wheelchair's frame, quickly telescoped it out and flicked a switch that turned it into a four-foot Taser.

He took out two of the gang members with the Taser, and they both fell to the ground twitching and moaning. Two gangbangers turned to run but were quickly cut off and caught by the cruisers pouring into the lot, now with lights flashing.

Jerome alone remained, staring down at Skeeter. He looked back up at Tonya and charged her, yelling, "You hurt Skeeter, bitch!" Tonya dislocated his left kneecap with a well-placed sidekick and he went down hard, screaming in agony.

After the gang was rounded up, cuffed and taken away, and Tonya and George had answered the requisite questions for the VBPD sergeant, they finally rolled and walked the remaining thirty feet to Tonya's car.

"You were smooth, Ton," said George. "Like a lioness."

"Thanks, George. You did great, too. A taser, for real? That thing legal?"

"What taser, baby girl?" She looked and could not find the Taser rod he had re-inserted into the frame of his wheelchair.

"Stealthmobile," she said, and they both laughed. She bent down to hug him and give him a chaste kiss goodbye on the cheek, but he moved her mouth over to his and she let him kiss her.

She felt a stirring she had not felt in a long time, but she put her hands on his shoulders and pushed away, breaking off the kiss.

"You are something, George Johnson. I think you're the

smooth one. And thanks for a fun night. Not many girls can say their date took them out for a mugging!"

She got into her car to the sound of George's laughter while he rolled across the parking lot, back to the boardwalk to play a few tunes for the tourists.

19

July 10, 7:37 a.m.

63rd Street

Virginia Beach

MICHELLE WAS SWIMMING ALONE at night, beyond the break at Rick's beach on 63rd Street. The ocean felt great. She loved the feel of it gliding by her as she stroked and kicked her way rapidly through the water. It was invigorating and fulfilling, and she often did some of her best work after a swim.

Swimming had been one of her sports in high school, and it was still one of her favorite ways to relax. Then there was Rick, she thought to herself with a smile. They released a lot of pent-up energy together cycling through Seashore State Park, racing their matching Seadoos, and through their lovemaking, what Rick liked to call their "horizontal workouts."

Suddenly, she felt a powerful change. A rip current! Michelle had been caught in rip currents before, so she didn't panic, but went with it, swimming perpendicular to the beach.

Soon she was swept away from shore, and the lights from the houses behind the dunes were rapidly receding. This couldn't be right, she thought. Normally rip currents end fairly quickly after you swim out of the neck of outrushing water, but this one seemed to be getting stronger the farther out she got, and she couldn't seem to clear it.

She was getting tired and decided to float on her back for a while. The current continued to pick up speed and soon she was moving so quickly across the water a wake appeared behind her, with phosphorus sparklers streaming from her feet and hands. It was mesmerizing to see and, in spite of her predicament, she stroked her arms across the water to watch the phosphorous streaks follow her movements—like making snow angels in the snow. It was magical.

Then she turned onto her stomach and arched her back like she was bodysurfing. The current was really pushing her along. She figured she was doing at least 10 mph, and still heading out, away from the beach. There was nothing she could do about it. Then she saw the fins. There were three, and all of them were keeping up with her, sometimes diving under and over to the other side, sometimes behind and sometimes disappearing for a moment, but always coming back to swim in tight formation with her.

She couldn't tell for sure, and she hoped and prayed they were dolphins, but they sure *felt* like sharks. Her spirit and her body became suddenly cold and dark.

Then a bright beam of light lit the scene, and from the middle of the light she could hear Rick's voice calling to her, "Wake up Michelle, you're dreaming. Wake up." She opened her eyes and smiled up at Rick, who was sitting on the side of the bed with a worried look in his eyes. "You saved me from the sharks," she said softly as she sat up. He handed her a cup of coffee and she gratefully took it, the first sip warming her body, which had turned cold from the water in her dream. He noticed her shivering and wrapped a blanket around her.

"You wanna tell me about your dream?" Rick asked.

"No," she replied dreamily, "I'm good. I'm not going to die by shark." She smiled up at him and, as usual, it took his breath away. They had been dating for about a year and had become quite comfortable. Neither was in a hurry to alter the balance or take the next step. They kept their independence, but enjoyed sharing leisure time and working together.

Like the current case of the Russian maids.

Michelle had been dreaming about the murders and the killer over the past few days, as she began putting together a psychological profile that could help them determine the motive, age and behaviors of the killer. Her waking thoughts and nighttime dreams, however, were beginning to overlap, she sensed a picture of the murderer slowly coming into focus.

"I've got breakfast ready, Madam Dreamcatcher," said Rick, walking back to the kitchen. She stretched, got up, and went about her morning regimen. She finished eating the tasty vegetarian omelet Rick had fixed, along with fresh-squeezed orange juice and blueberry yogurt. She stared out the window at the pampas fronds blowing gently in the breeze and thought again about her dreams.

"He's committing suicide, Rick."

"Who is?" asked Rick, looking up from *The Virginian-Pilot* newspaper he had been reading.

"The bad guy," she said, taking another sip of her coffee. "I think he's making a last will and testament with the murders, and there will be more. In a sad, strange way, he's reaching out to us, hoping to be understood."

"How can he expect to be understood by committing murder?"

"He doesn't see them that way, Rick. To him he's creating beauty and art. He's sharing his art with the world and using these girls as his canvases. This is a very complex man we're up against. He's smart and sophisticated. And he's probably rich."

"Yeah, I agree on the rich part," said Rick, pouring himself another cup of coffee, clearing the dishes and washing the pans. "Just being able to pull off the Magritte ID theft alone cost a bundle. And he probably paid at least ten grand to get the credit card and Canadian passport made. I'm glad we got the Fibs on that angle. What else do you see in this guy?"

"He likes to make things, and is good at managing complexity. He's probably a successful businessman. Educated for sure, loves history, and he obviously loves art. Are you guys checking out that angle?"

"Yeah, we're looking at art school graduates who've gone into business on the East Coast. Slow going. How old do you think our guy is?"

"The energy I've felt at both scenes is strong and it has an edge, but it's also very controlled. This is not an impulsive kid, that's for sure. It takes a while to create that kind of energy and confidence. I'm thinking he's at least 40, but no older than 60. So say 50 is our target age. That sounds right, because you guys said he's still in good shape. But whatever his age, he has boundless, relentless energy."

Rick took off the cooking apron she had bought him for his birthday last year, and walked up to her. A telltale bulge told her that his mind had wandered while they talked.

"How's my energy, mam?" he asked, hands on his hips.

She laughed and grabbed his crotch, pulling him closer. "I can't be sure, Mr. Jameson, until I do a thorough reading. Perhaps we should retire to my private office?"

20

July 11, 9:20 a.m.

VBPD Second Precinct

Virginia Beach

KELLY WILLIE WAS STALKING her prey, and once again it was the Dapper Detective, Lt. John Ordberg. Thanks to the recent phone conversation she'd had with her father, the chief of police, she knew Ordberg was heading for a meeting with the mayor at 10:30. Part of her hated to take advantage of her dear old dad that way, but she also loved how she could manipulate him into giving her virtually whatever she needed.

She had him wrapped around her little finger. It had been that way since she was a little girl, the apple of his eye, his little princess. He had given her everything she wanted, especially after her mother died, the victim of a horrendous car accident.

Educated at Norfolk Academy, one of the best private schools in the area, she had her own horse and riding lessons when she was 12, a new car when she turned 16 and papa also sprang for five years at Regent University, where she finished her fast-track Masters degree in Communications.

WAVY-TV had been impressed by her intelligence and her looks, and gave her a break with one of their community programs. She had turned it around in six months and made it a moneymaker, warranting the bump to a daytime slot. Within a year an opening occurred at the 5:00 news rotation, and she quickly took over as a newsbeat and crime reporter. Her style was so fresh she became known as a "Geraldo" style reporter, armed with inside information and leading questions that disarmed her subjects.

Ordberg was a tough one to crack, and so far she'd gotten nowhere with her interviews of the man. But she had much better luck with the hotel employees, including the Poseidon manager, Pratt, who had been so bedazzled by the camera and lights in Kelly's eyes, he had divulged a treasure trove of details about the scene.

Then there was her new "boyfriend," Mick Gorbach, Rick Jameson's trusted sidekick. She had met him soon after the first murder. He was good-looking and charming, with a slight Russian accent and an upbeat manner. It had been an easy task to reel him in, she thought. Now she was pumping him for information, and all she had to do was let him pump her in return. She smiled at the memory of last. Perhaps there would be more to this relationship, she thought as she called him.

"KGB!" Mick answered with a thick Russian accent.

Kelly laughed. "Hello, I'm looking for the famous spy, Michael Gorbachev. I have something he may have left behind."

"And what might that be, my delicious Americanski girl?"

"My panties," she replied in her most seductive voice.

There was a pause on the end of the line, and then Mick

cleared his throat, coming out of his spy character and back to the present. She had him!

"Damn, Kelly," he said, "I think you won that conversation. What can I do for you or... with you?"

"Tell me more about Ivanov and his boys. I'm planning on interviewing him later today and I'd like something I can throw at him. Something that will startle him."

"Kelly," replied Rick in a more serious tone, "You be careful with Ivanov and his 'boys' as you call them. He is a very big shark and he will eat you up if you're not careful. His guys are as tough as they come, and Nick's got an entire battery of lawyers covering his ass."

"Oh, I'm not going to start off with that stuff, Mick. The interview is being set up so he can let the world know how heartbroken he is about the murders of his two employees." She saw Ordberg walking out of the Second Precinct, heading for his car. "Rick, I gotta go! Ordberg's coming out."

She pointed to Ordberg while she touched up her makeup on the visor mirror, and Roger, her uplink tech and driver, gunned the van over to Ordberg's car, blocking him in. Kelly jumped out along with her cameraman, Sam, who handed her the wired microphone as she positioned herself in front of the smiling Ordberg.

"Live in five-four-three-two...." said Sam, his camera in position.

"This is Kelly Willie, live at the Virginia Beach Police Department's Second Precinct with Lieutenant John Ordberg, the lead investigator of the Special Task Force covering the murders." Sam zoomed the camera out to include Ordberg, as Kelly turned to the Detective.

"Lieutenant, I understand a task force has formed and that the city is bringing in the FBI to help solve the case. Is this serial killer beyond the abilities of your department?"

"Not at all, Ms. Willie. We're quite capable, but not above asking for extra help, the kind of help the FBI can provide. It would be like your station asking NBC national in New York to send down some folks to assist you with the story. In fact, I believe that's already happened, correct?"

Kelly was momentarily thrown off by Ordberg's turning the tables on her. It was true that national had sent a crew, along with CNN, FoxNews, MSNBC and others. She was under the spotlight, and she planned to make the most of it.

"Big Brother is always welcome," she said with a disarming smile. "Lieutenant, is there a connection between the Russian mafia and the murders?"

"The only connection we have at this point is that both women were Russian maids working at local hotels and employed by Tsarina Enterprises..."

"Which is owned by Nikolai Ivanov," finished Kelly. "There is speculation that Ivanov's past history with the KGB and the Soviet military led to involvement with the Russian underworld. Isn't it true that Ivanov has built an illegal crime network that exploits the very same Russian maids and puts them to work in prostitution?"

"Mr. Ivanov is not under investigation for the murders of the two women," replied Ordberg, deadpan.

"But are you investigating him for prostitution and other crimes?"

"I really can't speculate about other investigations the department is conducting, Ms. Willie. What I can tell you is that Mr. Ivanov is not a suspect in these murders."

"The woman who was murdered in the Poseidon worked for Mr. Ivanov as a maid, but isn't it true she was also working in Mr. Ivanov's escort service and had been hired for sex by the killer?"

"Sheer speculation, Ms. Willie."

"But possible?"

"All things are possible." He turned to the camera. "If anyone has any reliable information about this case, please call the Second Precinct. Thank you, Ms. Willie, and good day." With that he walked to his car, where he waited as Willie wrapped up the interview and the equipment was loaded back into the van. Kelly approached Ordberg with her sweetest smile.

"Thanks again for the interview, Detective," she purred.

Ordberg smiled. "You're quite welcome, Ms. Willie. Congratulations on your coverage of the case. You really are quite good at this, aren't you?"

She blushed with pride. "Thanks, Lieutenant. May I call you John?"

"I think not," replied Ordberg with a smile. "Not when we're both wearing our work uniforms."

"What if we're out of uniform?" she asked in a breathy imitation of a sexpot, placing her hand on his arm.

Ordberg laughed. "I'll let Mick handle those after-work matters with you, Ms. Willie. In the meantime, I'm sure I'll be seeing more of you."

"As much as you want, Lieutenant," she said brazenly. Then she turned and got into the waiting van and drove quickly away. Ordberg knew she was teasing him, and it took every ounce of his willpower to avoid taking the bait. What a woman, he thought, as he left for the meeting with the mayor.

God, I love this car, he thought, losing himself to the power and speed of a perfectly built automobile.

21

July 11, 10:30 a.m.

Mayor's Office, City Hall

Virginia Beach

THE OFFICIAL TASK FORCE assembling at the mayor's office had grown to ten people, including offsite support technicians and staff. Local law enforcement was represented by Ordberg, Jackson, Michelle Paige, Captain Rogers and Chief Willie. Grigorevna and two other FBI agents added to the show. Craig Hansen, CEO of Hospitality America, and Bill Mackey, representing the Virginia Beach Hotel Association and the Oceanfront business district, rounded out the card.

Mayor Bill Stevens was the consummate politician and had—by most accounts—been a decent mayor for the past eight years. Now he was working hard on a run for Congress, and every move he made was carefully considered in terms of its net public relations benefit.

After the introductions were made, Stevens called the

meeting to order. "Okay, Chief," he said to Willie, "Before you tell us how your team is doing, I've asked Craig and Bill to fill us in on the current situation down at the Oceanfront." He turned to Hansen. "Craig, it's all yours."

Hansen took the laptop's remote and walked to the front of the room near the screen. He brought up the first image, which showed an aerial photo of the Oceanfront area from Rudee Inlet to the end of the Boardwalk, around 40th Street.

"Ladies and gentlemen," he said, nodding toward the image, "The two murders this city has experienced affect the very lifeblood of our tourism industry. Numbers revealed the high percentage of tourism dollars in the city's annual budget.

"Every year the Beach gets around fifty million in net direct revenue tax— from about a billion dollars in gross revenue— from Oceanfront hotels, motels and other support businesses, including restaurants and shops. That's billion with a big 'B.' Imagine what could happen if the bookings dropped even ten percent. You're looking at not just lost sales, but lost revenue from taxes that could affect schools, roads and all other items on the city budget, such as our finest, the VBPD. No one wants that."

"You're damn right we don't!" barked the mayor, looking around the room. "We can't afford it and I won't have it. Go ahead, Craig."

"Just after military and the service/retail sector, tourism is the third-largest contributor to the Virginia Beach economy and budget, and supports more than 15,000 tax-paying employees."

"Damn right they do," said the mayor, rising from his seat and gesticulating toward the display. "Thanks, Craig." He grabbed the remote and commanded the floor. When all eyes were on him, he played the crowd.

"Folks, these murders are a significant threat to our fine city. I can't overstate that fact. The current situation is threatening the livelihood of thousands of employees as well as the vacations of so many tourists who come to our wonderful beaches."

"What a crock of shit," whispered Jameson to Ordberg.

"Do you have something to share, Mr. Jameson?" asked the mayor with a frown.

"Yes, sir," replied Jameson with an innocent expression. "I was just telling the Loo what a crock of shit it would be if people lost jobs and tourists couldn't come to play on our fair beaches because of these shitty murders. Sir."

Ordberg closed his eyes and waited for the bomb to drop. All eyes turned to Mayor Stevens, who continued to stare at Jameson as conflicting emotions and colors played across his face, finally settling on pleasure and a slightly flushed look.

"Yes, Mr. Jameson," he finally offered, nodding his head. "Well said. It would be a shame if one man could control the destiny of so many, and we will not stand for it—no we will not. We need to protect our citizens and our vital tourism industry and get this monster off the street."

"But we don't have to protect the maids," Jameson mouthed to Ordberg, who kicked him under the table.

Fortunately, the Mayor was so puffed up by his own rhetoric that he didn't notice. He ceded the floor to Chief Willie, saying, "Your show, Chief. What precisely is being done to find this 'crock of shit,' as Mr. Jameson so eloquently coined him?"

The Chief paused and looked at the people around the table. "Sir," he began, "With all due respect to Mr. Hansen and Mackey and their need to represent the Oceanfront, I'm not comfortable with sharing forensic evidence and the intimate details of our case with them."

"So noted, Chief," replied Mayor Stevens with a smile, "But I want them to hear how well the city is handling the case. We don't want panic, Chief. We need calm assurance and steady-as-she-goes. Please continue."

The Chief spent the next few minutes laying out the bones of the case and answering questions, while Ordberg and Paige filled in background information and showed supporting graphics and video footage. The case was complex, and the investigation had many moving parts. While there were some promising leads, there were no breakthroughs as of yet.

"So basically we've got nothing at all, Chief, is that what you're telling me?" sniped the mayor following Willie's summation.

"No sir." The chief was unfazed. "I'm not telling you that at all. We have not yet solved this case, certainly, but we *are* putting together an excellent profile on the killer; the forensics evidence is beginning to come together, and we are pursuing multiple leads. These things take time."

"We don't *have* time, Walter," said the Mayor.

"Ms. Paige," said Craig Hansen, who had remained silent until then, "I've studied some of your profiles from earlier cases. Very impressive work."

Michelle found it difficult not to be flattered by the charming man across the table. She knew of Hansen and his many hotel projects at the Beach and elsewhere around the country. He was reputed to be closing in on breaking 'the billionaire barrier,' was in good shape for his age, and had a long list of women who wanted nothing more than to be on his arm and in his bed. She was attracted to his charm but also realized something about him gave her the creeps. "Thank you, Mr. Hansen."

"Please call me Craig. All my friends do. Can you share the profile you've developed on the killer so far? What's in your report seems to just scratch the surface. I know what a psychological profile looks like, so even I can guess something of what this guy must be like. Because it *is* a guy, is it not?"

Michelle turned to Ordberg, who turned to the chief, who glanced briefly at the nodding Mayor and said, "Go ahead, Michelle."

"Yes, Mr.... Craig. We believe the killer is a white male, approximately 50 years of age. He is extremely intelligent and well educated. He has received art training and has excellent skills in that area. He may have also had training in theatre or film production, which would explain his use of props, sets and makeup, and his penchant for elaborate sets."

"What about the women?" asked Hansen. "Does he love the women he kills?"

"He thinks he loves them and expresses his sociopathic love for them by using them in his life paintings."

"What a wonderful way to put it. So he does love them?"

"No, Mr. Hansen, the killer does not love women. He hates them and desires to degrade them. He is a sick and twisted sociopath without a shred of remorse."

Hansen continued to stare at Michelle after her reply, and the red color rising on his neck gave proof that he had not liked her answer. They stared at each other for a beat.

Finally the mayor slapped the table and stood. "Great work, people. Chief, keep me posted. Craig, see you tonight at the event. Can't wait." With that, he shook hands all around, posed for some pictures, and left with his staff in tow.

Hansen approached Michelle and Rick where they stood talking with Ordberg and the rest of the team. "The mayor mentioned the fundraiser tonight. It's a fashion show at

Maxima, and Brandy really knows how to put on a show. Of course, it helps that I'm underwriting the event!"

He took Michelle's hand in his and lightly kissed it, saying, "Why don't you come—as my guest?" He turned solicitously to the others. "Shall I send a limo for you all at, say, 8 o'clock?"

"We have a lot of work to do on the case, Mr. Hansen," said Ordberg.

"Your friend Ivanov will be there Lieutenant, along with many beautiful Russians. I think this may be in keeping with your work, don't you?" He shook Rick's hand last and said, "Besides, Michelle needs a night out, Rick, don't you think? You're a bourbon connoisseur, right? I've got a bottle of 16-year-old A. H. Hirsch Reserve as a gift for you."

His charm and powers of persuasion were such that Rick and Ordberg were befuddled. Maybe this *was* a good idea. Anyway, what could it hurt, *and* it would be a chance to see Ivanov and his Russian girls in action.

Seeing the change in Ordberg's expression, Hansen clapped his hands and said, "Excellent, I'll send the limo to the Precinct at 8 o'clock, sharp."

22

July 13, 8:15 p.m.

Oceanfront Poseidon

Virginia Beach

THE HUMMER SUPER-STRETCH limo picked them up precisely on time and drove the length of the Atlantic Avenue strip while drinks were served by a white-gloved waiter whose front bucket seat swiveled 360 degrees, giving access to a full bar and all guests. After he served them, he closed the dark Plexiglas screen divider and sealed the team in soft Bose-caliber music and luxury.

All the seats and the three couches were covered in soft leather, each with its own monitor, currently showing a closed-circuit satellite link of the pre-show party going on at the Poseidon.

"Check that out," said Tonya, pointing to one of the screens, "We got the fashion show on a live feed. I vote we cruise around in the limo and have our own private party on wheels!" A chorus of agreement rose from the others, with the exception of Ordberg, who stared out the window, watching tourists walking by on the sidewalks, gawking at the giant limo.

Ordberg glanced back at Tonya and quipped, "It would seem you are already having a party on Wheels, Ms. Tonya." The others laughed at Ordberg's word play, as Tonya straightened up from where she had been leaning against Wheels. Since the kiss in the parking lot, things had changed between them, and they had started getting more physical. She had not even been aware of the contact in the limo.

Ten minutes later they turned into the Poseidon's driveway, where a large tent and red carpet gave the glint of Hollywood, complete with camera crews and satellite trucks from two local stations as well as CNN.

"Drive around to the parking deck," Ordberg ordered the driver.

"Mr. Hansen said to drop you off out front," replied the driver, pulling the limo over to the red carpet.

Ordberg took out his badge and slapped it against the cheek of the driver, then held it up in front of his eyes. "My gold badge says drive us around," he said quietly, "And if you don't do it quickly, my friend here in the wheelchair will fall out in front of your limo. That would be a terrible end to your career."

The driver seemed to get it, and dropped them off on the second floor of the parking deck. As they crossed the pedestrian bridge over to the Poseidon, Rick said, "Good one, Loo. Who knew you had a sense of humor?" They all laughed, especially Wheels.

The loud, thumping pulse of Euro-Technica music assaulted them as soon as they entered the Poseidon's second-floor ballroom. They paused for their eyes to adjust to the dimness, strobes and revolving disco balls. A thirty-foot raised runway split the room, where a crowd talked and danced, suspended above the fray. All around the walls and positioned throughout the room were mannequins wearing the latest frou-frou fashions.

A bar at each corner kept the booze flowing and tuxedo'd servers circulated platters of heavy hors d'oeuvres, including caviar, sushi and assorted fruits, cheeses and sweets. Others poured Cristal champagne into fluted glasses.

"My Lord!" said Michelle as the team walked the length of the runway, "I thought this was a fundraiser. Each bottle of Cristal must cost a couple hundred dollars. Who pays for all this?"

"That would be our local billionaire, Mr. Craig Hansen," replied Rick.

A group of gorgeous, laughing women suddenly surrounded the team, mesmerizing the men and charming the women. They were obviously models for the show, judging by their makeup, cover-girl beauty and Russian accents. Elena instantly connected with the Russian women, and they chatted happily in their native language while the party swirled around them.

Michelle got caught up in the same circle of women, and they were both swept away by dancing Russians. They snaked their way through the crowd, and over to a raised platform where the DJ was spinning tunes. Nikolai Ivanov, Brandy West and Craig Hansen were there, holding fort.

The Russian models deposited Elena and Michelle beneath the platform, blew kisses to Ivanov and danced their way into the crowd. Elena gave Michelle a sarcastic smile and said, "I feel so used." She stepped up onto the platform with help from Ivanov, while Craig Hansen assisted Michelle.

A server bearing champagne materialized out of nowhere, and Hansen proposed a toast, "To Michelle, the dream-catching psychologist." Soon Ivanov and Elena were chatting away in Russian before the uncomprehending Brandy West, who went to check on preparations for the show. That left Michelle alone with Hansen, a not completely unpleasant task, she thought. He was clearly interested in her, but she was not sure how she felt about the intensity of his focus.

He noticed. "You're wondering about my sudden interest in you, right?"

She laughed and the tension she'd felt evaporated. "Maybe I was wondering why you'd be so interested in me when you're surrounded by beautiful, young Russian models. I've seen them looking at you. I'm just a plain American girl."

"No, Michelle, you are anything but plain. You are a work of art, a masterpiece."

She blushed and asked, "Why are you so interested in the killer's profile?"

"I studied some psychology in school, way back in the day."

"Oh, where did you go to school?"

"VCU, but I didn't major in psychology. I dabbled in various subjects, including business—even a little art." He nodded toward Rick and Ordberg, who were being escorted through the crowd by a coterie of models. They changed direction when Brandy shooed them toward the back of the runway.

"Looks like the show is about to begin. We need to take our seats." He helped her down from the runway and handed her off to Rick with a small bow. "Thanks for allowing me the pleasure of Michelle's company, Mr. Jameson."

"Call me Rick, and you're welcome. Thanks for having the Russian girls cut us off so you could spend time with Michelle. Very clever!" They laughed and took their seats as the house lights dimmed and floodlights lit the runway.

Sergei had watched Michelle for most of the night and, as she took her seat, he realized that he was lost in a fantasy in which she was the star. He had already planned his next masterpiece, but the canvas was completely blank after that. He was jealous of the men she was with, especially Rick. He thought about various ways he could destroy him. Perhaps a double body-art piece?

The more he thought about Michelle, the more he loved the idea of her as the subject of his art. How would he set her and dress her? Something spiritual? Yes, but not religious. A fortuneteller and her crystal ball, perhaps, with maybe a gypsy flavor mixed in? He laughed at the thought as he found a seat and settled in to enjoy.

23

July 13, 10:36 p.m.

Poseidon parking deck

Virginia Beach

ELENA GRIGOREVNA WALKED UP the ramp to the top deck of the Poseidon's parking garage and stood at the wall near her car. She paused at the edge, looking down at the brightly lit boardwalk and beyond to the boats and ships on the Atlantic. A breeze blew her hair; it had been a pleasant night, she thought, in spite of the nature of the investigation. She knew enough to take pleasure whenever it showed itself.

She was sure that Ivanov was running a prostitution ring with Brandy West, and some of her D.C. specialists had assembled the financial evidence to prove it. Ivanov was clever and careful, but West was sloppy with her records. She would probably be the downfall of the operation. Which was why she had arranged this meeting with Brandy— to offer her a deal to build a solid case against Ivanov.

She turned at the sound of heels click-clacking their way up the ramp from the lower level. Elena noted how Brandy still moved with the poise and care of the model she once was.

———————

Boris and Jessie watched Elena from inside the heavily tinted vehicle they had parked within 25 yards of her car. They had easily tracked her using the GPS transmitter Boris had slapped on her car while she working inside the Second Precinct last night.

"That the FBI bitch?" asked Jessie.

"Da," said Boris. "Boss wants us to know what she know."

"I don't like messing with the Feds."

"You shut up and do as told, you make much money."

"What the fuck she waiting for?"

As if in reply, Brandy West walked up to Elena and they began talking together in a conspiratorial manner.

"Oh shit," said Boris.

"What?" asked Jessie, "Who the fuck is she?"

"She Ivanov girlfriend."

"Oh shit is right."

Boris hooked up the long-distance microphone and attached it to a port in his phone. He called Ivanov and put it on speaker.

"Boss, you need to hear this."

———————

"Thanks for meeting me up here, Brandy," said Elena as Brandy approached her. "Sorry for the cloak-and-dagger stuff, but I don't want to get you in any more trouble."

"Any *more* trouble?" responded Brandy with irritation. "What are you talking about? Am I a suspect in these murders? I thought that's what you're working on."

"That is the main reason we came, Brandy, but not the *only* reason."

"What other reason could there be?"

"Prostitution."

"Oh, that shit again?" she snapped as she took out a cigarette and lit it. She paced now, her nervousness evident. "Cops have been trying to pin that shit on Nicky for years and he's always come out clean. So what's new this time?"

"We've found some damning evidence in financial records that should be enough to convict."

"Oh my gawd. Poor Nicky."

Elena grabbed Brandy's arm. "Listen to me, Brandy, I'm not talking about Ivanov, I'm talking about you. We have all your financial records and they paint a clear picture of complicity. You are the madam running the girls Ivanov provides you. We have you, Brandy. You are guilty. And you will go to prison for a long time."

Elena noted the range of expressions that flashed across Brandy's face—first defiance, then abject fear followed by terror then—finally—defeat. Brandy slumped down on the parking deck with her back to the wall, weeping uncontrollably. "He'll kill me."

Elena squatted down beside her and placed a hand on Brandy's shoulder. "We are close to nailing Nikolai to the wall, but we need your help. If you're willing to help us take him down, we'll make a deal with you."

"You don't understand. Nikolai will kill me!"

"We can protect you, Brandy."

Brandy slowly looked up into Elena's eyes with a defeated look. "Will I still have to go to prison?"

"No, not if we put you in the Witness Protection Program. You would probably have to wear an ankle monitor for the first year, but no prison. You would have to continue doing what you're doing and then testify against him. Those are your choices. Take it or leave it."

Brandy moaned, hugging herself and rocking back and forth. Then she stopped, composing herself. "Okay, I'll do it."

———————

A string of Russian curses came out of the speaker on Boris' phone. Even Jessie could figure out what some of the words meant. Boris disconnected the microphone and brought the phone back up to his ear, as Ivanov explained what he wanted in explicit detail.

"Da," he answered after Ivanov finished. They watched as Brandy walked back down the ramp and Elena got into her car and drove away. After giving the women ample time to exit the garage, Boris started the car, saying, "Boss not happy. We have work to do."

"No shit, Sherlock."

"Who is this Sherlock?"

"A dead detective."

"I like detectives all to be dead," replied Boris. They laughed as they pulled out of their space and slowly made their way back onto Atlantic Avenue.

24

July 17, 3:25 p.m.

Heritage Center

Virginia Beach

MICHELLE SMILED AND WAVED at Jenny, the young Heritage Center receptionist, as she made her way back to her office. She thought about the journey she'd taken to get to this place in her life, and once again pondered the irony of working for the police and "a bunch of spirit-filled crazy people," as Captain Rogers called anyone associated with the Heritage or the Edgar Cayce Center. She wished she had known Cayce, but he was before her time.

Edgar Cayce had moved to the Beach in 1925 and quickly gained a following for his transcendent readings and clairvoyant abilities. Virginia Beach became a New Age enlightenment center that catered to both locals and tourists interested in Cayce in particular and spiritualism in general.

From that sprang the Heritage Center and Store. The store

catered to the material needs of the retail customers – organic foods, vitamins, massage therapy and yoga classes. The center offered spiritual and metaphysical guidance, like meditation and psychic readings.

Ever since she was a child Michelle knew she was different. Her grandmother noticed, and told her that she, too, could "see" the special way Michelle did. It was like she could get inside of people and feel her way to the truth. This gift never felt spooky or strange to her.

She could often tell if people were lying, and she could interpret their dreams. She honed her intuitive skills and complemented them with a Doctorate in Psychology from the University of Virginia.

After clearing up some paperwork, she set about editing her profile of the Russian maid murders. The phone rang.

"Hi Michelle," said Jenny. "You are such a lucky girl! Oh my gawd, there must be like, 100 roses out here for you. Rick must be getting ready to pop the question! I'm bringing them back to you."

There were, in fact, 72 red roses beautifully arranged in an elegant ceramic urn. Michelle felt the hairs on the back of her neck rise as she reached for the note attached to the roses.

It read, "Dear Michelle, thanks for spending time with me at the fashion show. These roses are in hopes of more. With great admiration and respect, I am - Craig"

She felt as she had at the fashion show—flattered— strangely excited—and frightened. She couldn't quite put a finger on it. Michelle was not in the habit of purposely attracting other guys, but even as Rick conceded they couldn't help falling for her "great looks, hot body and holy spirit." He labeled all potential competition "assholes." She hoped Hansen would not become a problem. Again, the phone.

A woman's voice with a clipped British accent announced, "Please hold for Mr. Hansen."

"Hi Michelle, did you get the flowers?"

"Yes I did, Mr. Hansen, they're very beautiful."

"Please call me Craig."

"Craig, I have to admit that I'm a bit overwhelmed by your attention and interest in me. And you do realize that red roses are the color of passion and love? Are you in the habit of offering that to every woman you meet?"

Hansen laughed, and she found herself laughing along with him. He was infectious. "No, not every woman, but yes, the ones I am attracted to. I'm afraid I have a bad habit of making my intentions known quickly and sometimes too forcefully."

"So dating is like acquisitions and mergers, Craig?"

He laughed again. "Touché, Michelle, touché. Perhaps it is true. But I can assure you that all of my acquisitions appreciate and thrive from my attention and loving care."

"You do realize I'm in a relationship with Rick Jameson?"

"Yes, I am aware. I'm prepared to outbid and outplay him."

Michelle laughed. "Touché to you, Craig, but I'm very happy with my relationship with Rick. We're very close."

"I appreciate that, Michelle, I really do. I'm not trying to break you guys up. Quite the contrary. But for some reason I really like you and would just like to spend some time with you. That's why I'm inviting you and Rick to a little boat cruise August first."

"Somehow I doubt you do anything small, Craig. How big's your boat?

"157 feet. An ocean-going party with a prop. Sometimes

size really does matter, Michelle."

Once again Michelle found herself laughing along with Hansen, and agreed to discuss the trip with Rick.

25

July 20, 11:37 p.m.

15th Street fishing pier

Virginia Beach

MARENA WAS ANGRY, and it was all Klaus's fault. He had told her that he needed to see more passion, more heart—especially anger. She would have agreed just to make him happy, but what really inspired her was the $500 bonus he offered. He stuffed the cash into his shirt pocket, leaving it in plain view as a beacon. Easy money, she thought.

In the past she had done well relying solely on her unusual Eurasian beauty. Her modeling income increased over the past year and would soon eclipse her maid's income. Her dream was to give up the cleaning work and move to New York or Chicago or L.A. to pursue modeling full time. One day maybe she'd even get to do a shoot in Moscow and invite Mama and Papa.

The thought pleased her and she acted even angrier,

cracking the small black whip, snarling at the camera and clawing the air. She was every bit the pissed off cat woman, complete with black leather shorts and bra top, thigh-high fishnet stockings, high heels and the requisite black leather mask.

"Yes, baby, that's it!" urged Klaus. "Be my angry girl. Oooh, scratch me. Teach me a lesson. Yes....yes.....love the camera! Hiss for me."

Sergei could not remember the last time he had enjoyed himself as much as he had tonight. Never in a million years did he imagine he'd be doing a photo shoot of a beautiful cat woman at the end of a fishing pier. Yet here he was, exactly as planned, and what a plan it was.

Normally the pier was open for fishermen, and anybody who wanted to stroll out to the end and back—for a price—any time of the night or day. But in order to stage the shoot and then paint his scene, Sergei needed to own the pier for the entire night, which meant he needed to secure it from snooping tourists.

The manager, George Menten, had rented the pier to photographers before, as well as for the occasional wedding. But that was generally only for an hour or two, and the man known as 'Mr. Klaus' was asking for twelve hours, from six to six. The pier could take in $1,000 a night. So he set the price high and was surprised how quickly Klaus agreed to the $2,500 fee. He paid up front, in cash.

Klaus insisted on a uniformed security person at the pier entrance and full access to drive his van out onto the pier. All was going according to plan; wasn't life grand!

Compared to his previous performances, this set was quite simple. A beautiful red velvet backdrop served as a privacy wall and photo backdrop. On the pier's decking was a gigantic faux polar bear skin. Three male mannequins were arranged around the edges, each dressed as fishermen holding rods with real fish attached to the lines. Marena had complained about the smell, but he made her laugh when he began apologizing to the fish for Marena's complaints. After a while she forgot about the smell, and so did Sergei.

Marena didn't work as one of Ivanov's call girls, though she had been heavily recruited. The money was tempting, but her upbringing and the steady modeling income enabled her to reject the offers. Sergei respected that a great deal, and his respect would manifest in the pain-free death he would give her. He was practically giddy with delight as he captured hundreds of beautiful images on his Nikon D3. His three box lights lit the scene perfectly and Marena was positively glowing. He planned on posting some of these images online after the artwork was completed.

Sergei put down his camera and applauded Marena, who curtsied and waved to the tourists passing by on the boardwalk. She was really something, he thought, pulling out two ice cold Heinekens from a cooler. He handed her one and they clinked bottles.

"To making art," said Sergei.

"To making money!" Marena countered with a laugh.

"Funny you should say that." Sergei pulled cash out of his shirt pocket. He counted off five hundred dollar bills and handed them to her. "Here's the bonus money I offered you. You definitely have exceeded my expectations, Marena."

"My pleasure," she replied, then consumed half of the bottle in one long pull. "I'd like to take more of your money."

Sergei laughed at her boldness, loving her even more. "Yes, I'm sure you would, and I have more money than you could ever imagine." He pointed toward the line of hotels and said, "I could buy these hotels just for you."

She laughed and said, "Sure. And I buy this pier!"

He laughed along with her and said, "You are a businesswoman and I have a proposition to make. Would you be willing to pose in the nude for me, Marena? It will be tastefully done, I assure you, and you could leave the mask on."

Marena walked around the drop cloth and looked at the boardwalk, some 500 feet away. The cloth would shield her from view. Which just left the boats motoring by. A few curiosity seekers had already circled, but the pier obscured their view of the set, especially when she was sitting or laying down.

"Five thousand, just top off and I lie on bear so no one see me."

"Three thousand and you have a deal."

"Give me money first."

Sergei slowly counted off the thirty bills and gave them to Marena, and they disappeared into her purse. He grabbed his camera and pointed to the bearskin. "Time to love the bear, Marena."

Marena sat on the skin, looked up at Sergei and said, "You be good boy, Klaus. Look away." He did so. After she told him she was ready, he turned to find her topless and laid out in a titilating pose. Who knows, he thought, maybe he would win an award for this work? Look how beautiful she is!

He adjusted his lights and went to work; full concentration. She knew exactly how to pout and pose in sensual ways; his response was visceral and automatic. Marena noticed his erection as he moved over her with his camera, and waved her finger at him, repeating her warning, "You be good boy, Klaus!"

"Oh, I'll be good, mon cher, but I *am* a boy after all. I promise to keep my pants on!"

After firing off several quick frames, Sergei went to his van to change lenses. He also put a razor-sharp fishing filet knife in his back pocket. It was time to complete the art.

Marena noticed a change in Klaus as he approached her with the new wide-angle lens attached to his camera. She was immediately alarmed, and sat up tensely on the skin, covering her breasts. Her instincts took over. She stood, assuming the position taught her by Master Kim, her Taekwondo instructor. He had told her last week that he thought she could earn her black belt within the year, and she was working hard to get it.

Sergei loved her defensive posture, assuming she was doing it for theatre's sake, so he quickly grabbed several shots. "Lovely, Marena, really great," he said with admiration. "I love your tiger stance. Will you do another?"

"No!" she said, "Give me top!"

He stopped and it became clear that she knew what he was planning. Clever girl. He carefully set the camera down, and pulled the knife from his pocket without taking his eyes off her. She gasped as he moved in fast, making a lightning grab at her wrist. But she had trained for just such moves and instinctively blocked his arm, stepped to the side and then delivered a perfectly executed front kick to his thigh that rocked him back on his heels.

He changed his grip on the knife and attacked, coming in low, again trying to grab her arm while slicing the air near her throat. She blocked the knife with her forearm, taking a deep cut that immediately spurted blood onto the decking. She screamed, clawing his cheek with her nails, drawing blood.

"What the fuck?" George Menten walked around the backdrop, taking in the scene. He had not wanted to bother

Klaus during the shoot, but the police had come, complaining about the van on the pier and some stupid safety ordinance. George was a large man with army training. He instinctively stepped forward to protect the woman.

"Back the fuck away and put down the knife, Klaus!" Marena tried to run around Sergei but he blocked her against the back rails of the pier. He turned to Menten who had grabbed a backdrop support rod. "Let her go, buddy, or I will fuck you up!"

Menten swung the rod at Sergei's head. But Sergei had been expecting that move and ducked, stepping forward to plunge the knife into Menten's belly. He dropped the rod and stared at Sergei with a startled look on his face. "Please don't..." he whispered, as Sergei thrust the knife up into his heart, killing him instantly. Sergei pushed the body onto the bearskin and turned back to Marena.

Too late! She was straddling the railing and pushed herself backward over the edge, flipping Sergei her middle finger in salute. What a woman, he thought, as he heard her splash below him. He looked over the edge and could see her swimming toward the shore with strong strokes, despite her wound.

He retrieved his gun from the van and screwed on the custom-made silencer, but by the time he returned to the rail he could only see her legs as she disappeared beneath the pier. She had anticipated that he might have a gun. Clever girl, he thought again. Time to leave!

He abandoned his photo lights, the mannequins and the rest of the set—not to mention Menten's body—grabbed the camera and jumped into his van. He drove slowly to the gate and pulled up next to the security guard, rolling down his window.

"That looks like a nasty cut you got there, Mr. Klaus," said the guard, pointing to the bleeding wound where Marena had raked his face.

"Freaking photo light!" said Sergei, shaking his head. "Hurts like a bitch. Remember our deal, no one gets on the pier until 6 a.m. I'll be back tomorrow morning early to pick up the rest of the gear. This is for your trouble." He handed the man a crisp $100 bill and started to drive away, but the guard grabbed his arm.

"Where's that hot-looking model?"

"Oh, she'll be along shortly," replied Sergei. He drove slowly off the pier, on to 15th Street and out of sight.

He was worried about the girl being discovered so quickly and knew he had to move fast. But he was confident that once again his disguise and fake ID and fingerprints would throw off the police. He was disappointed about the artwork, but the more he thought about Menten stepping into the scene, the more he liked it. After all, he thought, one needed to be open for the sake of creativity. Once again he was amazed at how powerful he felt when he made his art. His life was his art and his art was his life. He was God's artist!

26

July 21, 1:15 a.m.

15th Street beach

Virginia Beach

AFTER KLAUS DROVE AWAY, the guard, Jeremy Wilson, went into the office just off the gatehouse to get a Coke and to let Menten know that Klaus had left. Menten was nowhere to be found, and since he had never come past Jeremy, he figured he was out at the end of the pier, talking to the model. What could it hurt if he strolled out and gave Menten the news and copped another look at the girl? Holy shit, she was hot!

About halfway down the pier he thought he heard a voice calling out, and went to the edge and looked down. Directly below him—in the water—was the model. She was trying to hold on to one of the pilings but the waves kept slamming her against it; her arm was bleeding and she looked exhausted.

"Help me, please," she cried out in a tired voice. "Please help me." Another wave hit her and she choked on the water, losing her grip on the piling.

Jeremy ran to the closest life ring, uncoiled the rope and tossed it over the side and away from the pier. "Grab it," he yelled down to the girl, "and I'll pull you into the beach." She swam out and grabbed the ring with both arms and he began pulling her to shore. She was heavy, he thought, and the waves made the going slow. Damn!

He stopped and pulled out his cell phone and called 9-1-1. Within three minutes he had five cops helping him pull Marena to shore. Two surfers had positioned her between their boards. As she was losing her grip, they pulled her up on one of the boards and used it as a floating stretcher. They paddled her to shore, where waiting paramedics wrapped her wound, and determined she was in no danger but was suffering from mild shock and hypothermia from the blood loss and water temperature. They put two blankets around her and gave her some Gatorade.

No one had gone to the end of the pier during the rescue, but when Marena repeatedly said, "He bad man. Bad man try to kill me!" while pointing out to the pier, the cops had walked out and discovered Menten's body, calling it in as a crime scene. The Task Force assembled.

While the forensics team went to work at the scene, Tonya, Michelle, Gorbach, Ordberg and Jameson descended on Jeremy Wilson, the security guard. Since they needed information quickly, Ordberg let Rick take the lead and use his NYPD methods.

"Helluva way to make a living, huh, Jeremy?" said Rick after introducing himself. "And nice going on the save. If not for you, that girl might not have made it. You're a hero."

Jeremy swelled with pride. "Hey thanks man. Just doing my job."

"You look like a cop. Did you serve?

"Yeah, here at the Beach, but I got busted out by a disability," he said, waving his arm, which was laced by stitches. "Tried to stop a bad guy and got run over. So I get a nice pension and get to do shit like this on fishing piers." They shared a laugh, and trust was established.

"So let me repeat what we got and what went out on the APB." Rick held up a sheet: "White Ford stretch Econoline van, recent model, clean. No signs, no markings. License PHOTOS. Nice work on that, Jeremy. Description of the perp, let's see...6 feet tall, maybe 200, well built. Medium-length dark hair and beard. Laceration on the left cheek. Wearing black T-shirt, black jeans, black boots and a black leather jacket. That sound about right?"

"Yeah, that's right, all in black. Hey, is this the same dickhead who killed the Russian girls?"

"We don't know yet. You're a cop, what do your instincts say about this guy?"

"I don't know. He was smooth as ice. Wasn't sweating or nothing when he drove up to me after killing Menten. Had that mean looking cut on his face; bet you a buck she's got some of his cheek under her nails. This guy was slick, I tell ya. Said he'd be back in the morning to pick up his gear. Slipped me a tip and drove off nice and slow."

"Aw, shit," said Jeremy when Rick held out his hand for the money. "I completely forgot about that. Here you go," he said, sliding the bill carefully into the open Ziplock bag Ordberg was holding up.

Tonya walked up. "Looks like our guy, Loo," she said. "We checked out the scene and got some basic info from the girl. Her name is Marena Fedotova. She's 22 and works at the Poseidon and models. Says he set up the shoot with her agency, Splash. He had brought by a cash deposit and everything seemed correct. He went by Klaus—only one name. Had a German accent but spoke good English."

"Make sure the techies check under her nails," said Ordberg. "Apparently she scratched his face pretty good." Tonya nodded.

"Maybe that will make him easier to spot," offered Michelle.

"I think not," replied Ordberg, "A little makeup goes a long way with this guy. Covering up a scratch should not be a problem for him. He was wearing a dark wig and beard, but his body type matches the description of murder one. For the moment we can assume this is our guy. What about the plates?"

Tonya consulted her iPhone and read, "PHOTOS, registered to a Mr. Keith Ranpher, Norfolk photographer. He reported stolen plates two days ago to Norfolk PD."

"Prints at the scene?"

"Loads of them," said Tonya, "but I'll bet you fifty bucks he used those new super-thin, clear latex gloves. Those things are like $200 a pop, but you can't even tell someone is wearing them. We're still running everything down."

"Lighting equipment—check with photo shops between here and Richmond for recent orders."

"On it," said Tonya. "And we're running the van to see if there've been any rentals in the past week. But as sharp as this guy is, I bet he's covered his tracks."

"Ladies and gentlemen," said Ordberg to the team, "we have had a break today. Our Mr. Menten was killed, but he interrupted the killing of young Ms. Marena, who spent a great deal of time with the killer. Michelle, would you be so kind as to lead the interview? I want to go a bit deeper with her."

27

July 21, 2:05 a.m.

Ammos' Restaurant, Sandcastle hotel

Virginia Beach

THE VIRGINIA BEACH RESCUE SQUAD wanted to take Marena to the hospital for a thorough checkup, but in the meantime, Ordberg had her taken to Ammos' Restaurant, which was close to the pier. He was friends with the owner, who agreed to shut down the restaurant for the interview. They had brought her coffee and scrambled eggs with cheese. After they brought her bag back to her, she dried and brushed her hair and put on some makeup

"Marena," began Michelle, "Lieutenant Ordberg wants to know more about the man who tried to hurt you."

Marena looked at Ordberg for a while, and said, "He kill other man with knife. I see this and jump in water. Cold water." She shivered and pulled the blankets tighter.

"Tell us about when he attacked you," directed Ordberg.

"He seem like photographer. He know what he do with lights and camera. He sound like photographer. But then he change and I knew he bad man."

"How did you know?"

"He wanted nude pictures of me."

"How did he talk you into it?"

"He give me much money and I felt safe, close to many peoples."

"So you were laying down and something changed. What was it exactly?"

"He go to van and fix camera. New lens I think. Small one. But when he come he look mean and I stand and fight him."

"How did you fight him?"

"Like this," she said as she stood. She pantomimed the moves in slow motion. "He try to grab wrist, I block and kick. He try to cut my face, I block with arm." She held up her arm and smiled. "I get cut." She sat again.

"Who taught you to fight that way, Marena?" asked Michelle.

"Master Kim teach Marena. Soon she black belt!"

Rick and Tonya exchanged a glance. Rick said, "Kim teaches Taekwondo at a dojo over on Birdneck. Excellent teacher. You are one lucky girl, Marena."

"I am alive and lucky, but that man not lucky and now he is died."

"Marena," began Ordberg, "Was there anything unusual about Klaus? Anything that stands out in your mind as different, not like other people?"

"Maybe yes. His hands and arms looks funny. Shiny. And he rich I think."

"Why do you think he's rich?

"He gave me much money and he say he buy me hotels. Not one but many hotels.

"Why is that important?"

"I believe him."

_____

After Ordberg assigned a uniformed officer to guard Marena, she was taken to Sentara Virginia Beach General Hospital for a complete physical and forensics examination. The team huddled to discuss the case.

"So the guy throws around money like water," said Rick. "We knew that. He's got a ready source of cash and he knows how to cover his tracks."

"He's getting sloppy," offered Ordberg.

"What makes you say that?" asked Gorbach, as he poured himself another cup of coffee.

Ordberg held up his hand and began counting fingers. "One, he didn't do his research on the new girl. He could have found out about her fighting skills. I think that surprised him and certainly saved her life."

"It didn't save Menten's life," quipped Tonya.

"And that would be the second point," said Ordberg. "It was sloppy to stage this murder in plain view."

"But the velvet drape hid most of the set," countered Tonya.

"True, but the entire set was like a beacon out on the end of the pier. He thought no one would suspect a crime would take place in plain sight. But it also increased the odds that something would go wrong, like Menten walking onto the set."

"What else?" asked Tonya.

"Three," continued Ordberg, lifting another finger. "He allowed himself to be marked in the fight, and did not kill his intended victim. We have a surviving witness."

"Four," said Michelle, "he's losing his artistic touch. This set pales in comparison to the other sets, and could represent the beginning of a breakdown or psychosis. That would be consistent with the selection of the venue. His sense of omniscient superpowers is growing, thus his behavior grows more bizarre and brazen."

"So what does that mean in the big picture?" asked Tonya.

"It means that the perp is becoming less careful and more random. It means he will do anything to get his way. He's starting to come apart. That means he's even more dangerous now and will start acting on his rage."

Tonya turned to Ordberg. "We better make sure Marena is protected—she's going to be unfinished business for him."

Ordberg reached for his phone, saying, "I'll add another uniform."

28

July 21, 3:30 a.m.

Sentara Virginia Beach General Hospital

Virginia Beach

SERGEI LISTENED TO THE CHATTER on the police scanner, waiting for the call. As he drove from the pier, his blood boiled and he was filled with a rage like no other he had ever experienced. That bitch! He knew she was a liability, not to mention that she was unfinished art and had to die. He knew it was risky, but he was way past caring.

"Unit 23, report to Beach Gen for guard duty of white female being transported by medical. Code 1. Confirm," came the call from the police dispatcher.

"Unit 23 copy. ETA 05."

Sergei arrived fifteen minutes later—still in his photographer's outfit—and asked for Marena Fedotova at the Emergency Dept. desk. The tired woman behind the counter consulted her computer. "She's just come in, and is in room 27. Are you related to her?"

"I'm her brother."

The woman filled out a stick-on badge and handed it to Sergei. "Put this on and go through those doors," pointing to the automatic doors behind her. Sergei did as he was told. He scanned the overhead signs and saw EMPLOYEE DRESSING ROOM. It was empty. He checked lockers for scrubs, but they were either empty or locked.

Then he found an open cubby with clean scrubs wrapped in plastic and ordered by size. He grabbed an XXL and put it on over his clothes. He found a cleaning cart, hid his gun beneath some wipes, grabbed a large floor mop, and headed out to find room 27.

He slowly mopped his way up the hallway toward room 27. A cop stood outside the door. Sergei pointed to where the cop was standing and—using a heavy German accent—said, "Please to clean there, sir?"

"You can't go in," said the cop. He pointed to the room and said, "No clean room!"

"No, just clean floor where you stand, sir."

Looking irritated, the cop stepped aside. Sergei picked up the wipes and his gun, stepped up and fired twice—through the wipes—into the cop's chest. Even with the silencer, a hissing spit of sound emanated with each bullet, and the brass casings echoed as they hit the floor. But he was in luck; no one was in earshot.

Sergei wiped down the blood splatter on the wall and floor, dragged the body into a nearby bathroom, and locked the door. He entered room 27.

Marena heard the sounds and was alarmed. She screamed as Klaus came through the door with a gun in his hand.

The bathroom door opened, striking Sergei's shoulder and knocking him backwards. Officer Hagen, the second uniformed cop, stepped out, wiping his hands with paper towels. A screaming Marena hurtled past him into the bathroom, slamming and locking the door.

She pushed the CALL NURSE button, yelling, "HELP ME! HELP! HELP!"

"What the hell?" said the cop, looking at the closed door. He turned to see Sergei raising his gun. Sergei shot him in the mouth, killing him instantly. He pulled the bathroom door handle.

"Come out, come out, wherever you are, Marena. Klaus is here to give you a present."

"Fuck you, Klaus!" yelled Marena.

Sergei heard footsteps running down the hall, coming his way. He stepped back and fired four times into the door, hoping to hit Marena. But he could hear her laughing inside the door. That bitch, he thought, why couldn't she just die like the others?

He ran out into the hall as two nurses and a large male orderly ran up. Sergei pointed into the room. "Looks like she locked herself in the bathroom." He walked quickly down the hallway. He heard screaming behind him, but by then he was out the door and running for his van. Damn that woman!

29

July 23, 10:32 a.m.

Tsarina Enterprises

Virginia Beach

"SHIT," SAID NIKOLAI TO GORBACH, Boris and Brandy West, "The cops can't do anything without stepping on their dicks. Two cops dead and another Russian girl almost killed—twice! So what are you guys gonna do to protect my investments?"

Boris nodded to Mick, who said, "We managed to pick up ten more guys with license to carry and security experience. Boris and I have set up a system so that each girl will travel with a dick."

"Girls have dicks?" asked Boris with a surprised expression.

"No, you imbecile," replied Ivanov. "It means detective."

"Ah, good. I want to be detective like Columbo. I see him on TV the other…"

"Shut the fuck up!" ordered Ivanov to a stupidly smiling Boris.

"The girls are scared," observed Brandy. "They don't want to work anymore since the killer is targeting Russians. I don't blame them, Nicky."

"I blame you, Brandy my sweet. I blame you if you don't make me money."

"I'm telling you they won't do it."

"Oh, they will do it, or they will have their visas pulled and get sent back home to a very dull life. But we don't want to do that, do we Brandy? No, of course not. So I want you to double their pay, and triple the charges for our clients."

"Are you crazy? No one will agree to those prices."

"Oh, but they will, my naughty bitch. Men are strange creatures. They want what is hard to get and expensive. Money is not an issue with our clients and they will pay whatever it takes to be with our beauties. Trust me on this. And do as I say."

He stood, saying, "I think that's it." They were dismissed.

As they were leaving, Mick said to Ivanov, "Mne nuzhno pogovorit s toboĭ."

"Mick, please stay and have vodka with me." They waited until Boris and Brandy walked out and shut the door.

"We have a problem," said Mick, switching to Russian, as Ivanov filled two shot glasses. "A big problem."

"We seem to be raining problems," replied Ivanov. "What is it?"

"Brandy is selling you out to the Feds."

Ivanov stood and looked down at Mick, willing himself to act surprised. "You better be real fucking sure about this, Michael Gorbachev. How do you know this to be true?"

"She met with Elena, the FBI chick, right after the fashion show. Elena told her they had the goods on her, enough to put her away for a long time. But if she agreed to help them bring you down, they would drop the charges and put her in the Witness Protection Program."

"And she agreed to this?"

"Yeah, she agreed."

Ivanov picked up the heaviest object on his desk, an expensive crystal decanter, and threw it against the fireplace, where it exploded into hundreds of shards. He then downed his shot in one gulp. He closed his eyes and breathed deeply.

"I find a shot of vodka and meditative breathing to be very calming at a time like this. So if this went down three days ago, why did you wait until now to tell me?"

"Elena wasn't talking, since this is a federal investigation, but she changed her mind today; said she needed us to protect Brandy in case this played a role in the murder investigation."

"You sure they got nothing on me?"

"Oh they got stuff on you, Nick, but not enough to convict. The Feds never move unless they have an airtight case."

"That, at least, is good news." He grabbed another bottle and poured himself another shot, standing and holding his glass up for a toast. Mick grabbed his glass as Ivanov said, "To Brandy, may she rest in peace, that bitch."

They consumed the shots. "Good work, Mick. Now go do some more good work for me!"

As Mick walked out one door, Boris entered from another and stood before Ivanov, who asked him, "Did you hear all that?"

"Yes, Boss, every word."

"So what do you think?"

"Rest in peace, Boss, that's what I think."

"Both of them, Boris."

Boris stared at his boss for a long while, then nodded his head.

"I want this one clean and impossible to trace. Both at the same time if possible."

"That may be tough, Boss."

"I think we better bring in Carlos for this one."

"Da. Good choice, Boss."

30

July 26, 4:25 p.m.

Princess Anne Road, near Pungo

Virginia Beach

"HI MICK," SAID BRANDY over the phone, "What's up *now*?"

"We need to meet, Brandy—now. Some shit is going down that could hurt you."

"No shit, Sherlock," replied Brandy with exasperation. "People are dying and I've got a shit storm raining on me, not to mention Nicky breathing down my neck. Tell me something I don't know, Micky."

"I'm not talking about other people dying, Brandy. I'm talking about you."

There was stunned silence on the other end of the line.

"Don't say anything more on the phone, Brandy. I'll pick you up at the store in twenty minutes and we'll take a drive to the country. Everything's gonna be okay."

Boris and Carlos smiled at each other after listening in to the conversation.

"Maybe not so okay," said Carlos with a laugh.

"Two bushes for one bird, right Carlos?" said Boris.

"What the fuck you mean?"

"They make easy for us, my friend," said Boris with a laugh, pulling out behind Gorbach's car.

It had been a simple matter for Boris to place GPS emitters on the West and Gorbach vehicles. They used a van with magnetic signs reading, "AAA Auto Service." That and their embroidered AAA shirts with name tags gave the perfect cover. In seconds Boris was able to attach the magnetic base inside the rear rocker panel of both cars.

Assembling the plastic explosives took a little longer, as they had to be molded and precisely placed by a demolition master like Carlos. He had driven down from Richmond the night before. By three o'clock both vehicles were rigged.

The trickiest part of the job was wrapping the remote steering device around the T-joint on the steering assembly. This would allow the remote in their trail car to control the steering. The material was highly flammable plastic and metals that would vaporize when the remote button was pushed to set off the charge inside the box. The unit was virtually untraceable; the accident wreckage would read as though it was caused by a simple failure of the T-joint. A terrible thing to lose your steering, thought Boris with a smile.

After picking up Brandy at her store, Mick had headed out toward Pungo, figuring a drive in the country would do them both good; maybe they could stop at Mungo's for a burger.

Earlier, Mick and Rick had discussed the situation and agreed Brandy was in considerable danger. Her options were to fess up to Ivanov and play the double-agent game like Mick, or pull out entirely and go into protective custody while they took Ivanov down. The evidence against him was piling up, aided by the testimony of a few Russian girls who had been convinced to help the case in exchange for not being deported back to Russia. The power of the Feds, he thought.

"So what's the big secret, Mick?" asked Brandy as they turned onto Princess Anne Road.

"Ivanov knows you been talking to the Feds."

Brandy couldn't breathe for several seconds, and her panic gave way to hyperventilation. Mick pulled over into a school parking lot and rolled down the windows.

"Breathe, Brandy. That's it. Slow down... good."

Brandy burst into tears. "Why does all this shit have to happen to me? I never hurt anyone. I'm just trying to make a living, Mick."

Mick eventually pulled back onto the road and continued toward Pungo.

Boris had been surprised when Mick pulled over, but his training kicked in and he drove past them, pulling in to a gas station on the next corner. Ultimately Mick's car passed them. After letting a car get in between them, he pulled back onto the road.

Carlos sat next to him, looking down at the remote control box in his lap. It had a small joystick in the middle, with arming toggles and a trigger button for each explosive, along with display lights indicating signal strength and readiness. He held it steady with both hands, lovingly rubbing the sides.

"This new system is amazing," he said to Boris. "With the old ones you had to be within 100 feet, but this one is good for a quarter mile. You could back off some if you want to, B-man."

"No, I'm good," said Boris.

Carlos pointed ahead, grinning. "Holy shit, look what's coming."

It was a huge gasoline tanker truck, a giant bomb on wheels, thought Carlos, laughing at the irony. This could not be any more perfect.

"Now maybe I pull back," said Boris, slowing down and pulling over onto the narrow shoulder. As they waited for the tanker to approach the target car, Carlos removed the covers and armed all three toggles, carefully holding the device between both legs and keeping his hands away from the steering joystick. The truck closed in.

———————

Mick looked at Pungo Pizza as they drove by and nodded to it. "Not a bad place to eat, and their Sicilian is excellent." He looked over at Brandy, who sat shell-shocked and silent. She had not yet decided what to do. Either way she felt trapped.

"Holy shit," said Mick, pulling the car slightly to the right. "Look at the size of that tanker. I'd hate to hit that thing. Can you imagine?"

Brandy looked up just as the wheel turned hard to the left. The last thing she ever saw was the astonished look on the face of the tanker driver as Mick's car ran head on into his grill.

At the moment of impact, Carlos fired both explosives. The smaller blast completely obliterated the steering remote and a good part of the steering rod. The larger explosive had been attached to the gas tank, and the initial spark of the explosion tore open the tank and ignited the vapors and the twelve gallons of gas; the destructive force of a 1,000-pound bomb.

The explosion raised the truck's front wheels off the ground, wrenching it hard to the right. The trailer jackknifed, taking out the two cars that had been driving behind Mick's vehicle and flinging them into the cornfields like one-ton Frisbees, instantly killing the drivers.

The tanker was filled with 9,000 gallons of unleaded high-octane premium gas. The bomb blast had been borne primarily by the cab, killing the driver and flattening his cab back and around both sides of the tank, which had miraculously not exploded.

But now a 100,000 pound, gas-filled tank was hurtling down the road at 40 mph. Mick and Carlos watched spellbound as the accident and explosion occurred, believing they were safe from their remote position 200 feet away. They were wrong.

"Back up!" screamed Carlos. "Hurry up!"

The tanker gained on them as Boris put the car in reverse and hit the gas. Unfortunately the shoulders were loosely packed with gravel and his wheels spun and lost their traction.

His front end swung over the deep drainage ditch that defined the road.

At the last minute, their left side tire gripped enough to pull them back onto the road. The truck continued to gain. "Faster!" shouted Carlos. But it was no use. The truck smacked them onto the front of the flattened cab. Carlos and Boris screamed as they flew backward. Four of the rig's left side tires blew out, tilting it—and the attached car—over onto its side. Fuel spewed from the tanker, which slowed and came to a stop, blocking both lanes of traffic.

The car was completely suspended from the front of the rig and canted at a 45-degree angle. Carlos and Boris were hanging suspended from their seatbelts, heads spinning and ears ringing. They were bleeding from multiple lacerations caused by windshield glass and other material that had flown off the truck.

"Owww, shit! We need to get out of here, Boris," said Carlos as he unbuckled his seatbelt.

Boris put his hands up just as the buckle snapped open. Carlos fell on Boris, and both fell against the driver's side door, which popped open, scraping the fuel-slicked road. The friction of the metal door against the asphalt was just enough to create a sizable spark, which ignited the fuel vapor pooling between the road surface and the tanker.

The resulting explosion could be seen as far away as the Norfolk harbor, some ten miles away, and the sonic wave was so loud that earthquakes, plane wrecks and—the favorite of the local police dispatchers—an atom bomb explosion were reported by frightened citizens. The tanker was obliterated; pieces of the chassis and the engine were hurled a quarter mile, but fortunately the area was agricultural, and the debris landed in open fields and wooded areas.

A 50-foot-wide, ten-foot-deep crater was carved out of the road and the fields on either side. It took rescue and emergency vehicles more than an hour to reach the scene as there were no other roads in. Some crews had to use 4-wheel-drive vehicles to off-road their way in across the fields. TV helicopters hovered over the scene for hours.

Based on eyewitness accounts from the two cars that had been behind the tanker, authorities determined that a large blue SUV with bike racks on top had crashed into the tanker, but no traces larger than a radio knob were ever found. The vehicle fit the description of Gorbach's, and Ordberg reluctantly realized both Mick and Brandy were killed in the accident. He knew they were meeting and Mick had mentioned Pungo. Horrible luck, he thought. Or maybe it wasn't a coincidence?

Boris and Carlos had remained undetected, both when their car was on the shoulder and after the crash. So no one knew there was a third vehicle involved until a week later when a farmer found parts of it in his soybean field, four hundred yards away.

No one except for Nikolai Ivanov. He had watched the entire crash live on Skype, transmitted from Boris' iPhone. He was delighted with the disappearance of Brandy and Mick. He would miss Boris, to be sure, and Carlos was irreplaceable, but now the slate was wiped clean again. He toasted himself with another shot of vodka and called for one of his girls.

31

July 27, 10:23 a.m.

Tsarina Enterprises, Town Center

Virginia Beach

TONYA JACKSON AND ELENA Grigorevna were escorted into Ivanov's office by two large Russians. Ivanov introduced his attorney, Eric Hester, and they sat at the small conference table.

"I'm sorry to hear about the deaths of Michail Gorbach and Brandy West," said Elena as coffee was being served. "I know they were friends of yours."

Ivanov shrugged. "Yes, they were my friends. It was a tragic accident."

"Really, how can you be so sure?"

"God only knows for sure; I am just guessing."

"Did you know we were talking with Brandy about your

prostitution business?"

"My business is employment!" yelled Ivanov.

"Not according to Brandy West. She told us everything, Mr. Ivanov."

"You have nothing, глупая сука [stupid bitch] !

Elena nodded to Tonya, who walked over to turn on the large monitor.

"What are you doing?" asked Ivanov.

"We want to show you something, Mr. Ivanov," replied Elena. "Officer Jackson is a bit of a computer hacker and, truth be told, I'd like to hire her to work with our office. She's done some outstanding detective work for us on this case."

"Congratulations, Officer Jackson. I'm sure this is a big deal for you and your people, but what does this have to do with me?"

"My people?" asked Tonya. "Just what exactly…"

"Officer Jackson," interrupted Elena, "Please pull up the website so Mr. Ivanov can see exactly why we're here." Tonya concentrated on her keyboard, hit a key, and her desktop was shown on the screen.

"What an impressive display of computer literacy," said Ivanov. "Do you also pick cotton in your spare time?"

"No, Mr. Ivanov," replied Tonya, "I picked the locks of your firewall." She hit another key and the words PRIVATE ESCORT SERVICE filled the screen, with fields for a user name and password.

Ivanov was silent, fury unmistakably etched on his face. Hester sputtered, "What is the meaning of this? I demand to…"

The FBI agent raised her hand peremptorily. "I suggest you watch and wait, Mr. Hester. This could affect you, too."

She nodded to Tonya, who typed in a user name and password. Photos and descriptions of over thirty beautiful young women filled the monitor. Next to each was a selection toggle and a GO TO CHECKOUT selection box.

"Who would you like to choose, Mr. Ivanov?" asked Grigorevna. "You know them all."

"No, I don't know any of these girls. I've never seen this website. This is bullshit!" He switched into Russian and began cursing Grigorevna, who said, "I'm liking the looks of Angelica. Mmm, what a nice name she has." She nodded to Jackson, and the screen changed to a photo of Angelica wearing a skimpy bikini, pouting at the camera. Ivanov continued to curse in Russian, while his attorney stared open-mouthed at him.

Tonya filled out the "order" using a credit card handed to her by Grigorevna, who noted, "We are ordering a night with Angelica. The card will be approved and will add to the evidence against you, Mr. Ivanov."

"This is not my website."

"You're right. The website is hosted by an underground company in the Ukraine, run by an old KGB friend of yours named Viktor Goronsky. As we speak, Ukranian authorities are paying him a visit."

Ivanov was restrained by his attorney, who said, "This is all very interesting and stimulating, Agent Grigorevna, but you have no proof my client was directly involved with this alleged prostitution ring."

"Proof? You want proof, Mr. Hester? Yes, I believe in having proof." She took a small radio from her bag and said, "Come." Within a minute, they heard the sound of yelling in the hallway, and the door burst open. Two of Ivanov's goons entered ahead of three FBI agents and Angelica, the woman from the website.

"Boss," said one of the goons to Ivanov, "I try to stop them, but they show me papers and guns."

The agents brought the white-faced Angelica over to the table, where she stood, looking down at her feet, tears streaming down her face.

Ivanov stood. "I don't know this woman!"

Angelica looked up at him and spat out a string of words in Russian, to which he responded in kind.

Grigorevna pointed at Ivanov. "You're right, Mr. Ivanov, she is a whore, as you say, and she has admitted it all to us. Everything. How the operation works, how you pick them, how often they've serviced you. We have money trails, bank accounts, customer names and credit card transactions."

"She is only one person against my word."

Grigorevna again lifted her radio and spoke, "Come again." The door immediately opened and four more agents escorted four more beautiful Russian models into the office.

"I believe you know these women, too, Mr. Ivanov. They are employed by Tsarina Enterprises with legitimate day jobs working as maids at local hotels, and you employ all of them as prostitutes at night. They are prepared to testify against you."

Ivanov lost it. He pulled out the gun attached to the bottom of the table and fired three times at Grigorevna, who was pushed back so hard against her chair from the force of the rounds that her chair careened into one of the agents. The agents had been surprised when Ivanov produced the gun, but by the time he fired his third round, three agents fired back at him.

The sound of gunfire was deafening. Ivanov was riddled with bullets. He was knocked backward, upending his chair and dumping him half crouched against the wall, looking quite shocked. He slid slowly down the wall, his blood painting it crimson, and died with his feet sticking up over the overturned chair. Blood spurted from his neck in an arc that splattered onto the table.

The Russian girls screamed as one and were removed from the scene by two of the agents. Another checked the pulse of the still-bleeding Ivanov, then checked his eyes. "No pulse, pupils fixed and dilated."

Grigorevna had been wearing a vest, which absorbed the impacts from most of the bullets, but sustained a wound to her shoulder. An agent placed a compression bandage on the wound and she stood, looking down at Ivanov. "Justice is served. Officer Jackson, would you be so kind as to call in your forensics team and seal this office? Thank you. Oh, and here's something that should help you get your gold shield. You can do the honors." She handed Jackson the arrest warrant.

Jackson approached the shell-shocked attorney. "Mr. Hester, you're under arrest for conspiracy to commit prostitution and mail fraud. You have the right to remain silent..."

32

August 1, 6:15 p.m.

Ritz Camera, Hilltop Shopping Center

Virginia Beach

FIVE TEAMS OF POLICE DETECTIVES and Elena's FBI team had been working the photo, art supply and theatrical leads for three days before they caught a break at a Ritz Camera in the Hilltop area of the Beach. Ordberg met Rick at the store and they went inside to interview the manager, Bob Smith.

He had been working on June 19 and recognized the sketch of the suspect. The man had bought an enormous amount of photographic gear that day; in fact it was the biggest single sale of the month. He had printed out the list.

"Let me guess," said Rick, "He paid cash."

"Yeah, afraid so," replied Smith. "Pretty unusual in this day and age but certainly welcome anytime."

"Holy shit, this guy bought a lot of stuff from you. Did he strike you as a photographic novice?"

"Oh no, he was a total pro. He knew exactly what he wanted, and he wanted the best. We had it all, for the most part, but the lighting kit was not quite up to his standards."

"So what's a pro act like?"

"Oh, I don't know. Usually they have a kind of swagger and artsy pretension about them. Plus he was doing the whole black-on-black thing, looking kind of like a Euro shooter. And he called himself Klaus and had an accent, maybe German. I remember that."

"So what'd he do with all the loot after he bought it?"

"Put it inside his van."

Rick and Ordberg shared a look. "Can you describe the van?"

"Looked like a Ford Econoline. I know, cause our region uses one. All white, and pretty new, I'd say."

"Why didn't you tell this to the officers?"

"They didn't ask and I didn't know it was important."

"Anything else you remember about the van?"

"Yeah, it had a snap-on license or something. Maybe it was held on by magnets but I noticed cause it was crooked. Really crooked. And there was a license under it that looked like it said AMER51. Not sure about the numbers, but I'm positive the first part was AMER. I like vanity plates, so that caught my eye."

Ordberg asked, "Were you able to see into the van?"

"Absolutely; I helped him load the equipment. It was completely clean. No gear, no dirt—I mean that sucker looked like it was right off the lot."

"Would you be willing to take a look at some photos of possible suspects?"

"You know I will, Detective."

Ten minutes later Rick and Ordberg waited in the Starbuck's near Dan Ryan's Clothing for Tonya to call them back; she was running the plates but the system had been squirrely and she was trying another route.

Rick sipped at his coffee while Ordberg stirred his cappuccino, both looking pensive.

"I remember a case in Queens," began Rick. "This guy was a master of disguise and always a mile or two ahead of us. Buttoned down, smart, impossible to catch."

Ordberg took the bait. "So how'd you catch him?"

"The dickhead comes into a deli with his old man's beard on."

"His dad wore a beard?"

Rick laughed. "No, Loo. He killed a girl wearing an old man's disguise, but in truth he was only about 30. It was an excellent disguise, as long as you had the whole shootin' match: the eyebrows, the beard, mustache and the hair. But for whatever reason he forgets to take off the beard and the guy at the deli starts laughing at the perp, who rips off the beard, runs behind the counter and stabs the deli guy."

"Did he kill him?"

"Hell no, just a scratch. Why would you ever go after a deli guy? They got the big knives and know exactly how to use 'em. He grabs the bad guy's hand, holds it down, and WHAM, cuts it off at the wrist with a meat cleaver! Guy about died from loss of blood, but he survived the trial and now does the one-hand jive at Attica."

"Now *that's* a story," said Ordberg, as his phone rang. He gave Rick one of his ear buds to listen in.

"You are not gonna believe this, Loo," began Tonya.

"Talk to me," replied Ordberg.

"AMER plus a number is the prefix used by Hospitality America."

Rick and Ordberg shared a glance, then Rick said, "You're shitting me, Tonya. Are you sure about this?"

"Absolutely sure. Our system was down at first so I called a friend and used DMV's. This is accurate, Boss. The only thing is they have not issued AMER51. They have a total of 44 vehicles registered with AMER and two digits. But check this out: AMER31—the 3 looks like a 5 from the bottom—was recently re-registered to a brand new, white Ford Econoline van, and it's waiting for us down at their Birdneck facility."

"Holy shit," said Ordberg and Rick simultaneously. "Tonya, ask them if they can get us photos of all their employees," said Ordberg.

"Already did. They have a photo album with all 789 employees listed. It's waiting for us at the Precinct."

"We need to round up..." began Ordberg.

"...the security guard, the Ritz Camera manager and the Russian model. Already did, Loo. Uniforms are picking up the model as we speak, and the other two are on the way. Be there by seven."

Ordberg and Rick looked at each other and smiled. "Damn, Tonya," said Rick. "You want the Loo's badge?"

"Hell no, I don't want that busted up old thing. I want my own shiny new one!"

"Right, I have a feeling it won't be long now, Tonya," said Ordberg as he and Rick walked out to their car. "Rick and I are on our way to the Precinct. Get Jacobs and Harrelson to cover the garage with the forensics team."

In the excitement, Rick missed the incoming call from Michelle, completely forgetting that he was due to meet her at Rudee Inlet for the trip out to Hansen's boat. The sharks were on the hunt.

33

August 1, 6:41 p.m.

Rudee Inlet fuel dock

Virginia Beach

"HELLO, YOU'VE REACHED the voicemail of Rick Jameson of Jameson Investigations. Please leave a message."

Michelle was surprised Rick didn't pick up, but she knew he was thick into some breaking stuff on the case. He was supposed to meet her here at the dock. A brand new 24-foot center-console Wellcraft was tied up in the slip, and Captain Bob was ready and waiting.

"Hey Rick," she said to the voicemail, "I'm down at Rudee and the boat's here. I'm going to go ahead and let him take me out to Hansen's boat. He said he'd come back for you. I want to meet the other psychologist Craig said was coming. See you on the boat, babe. Mwah!"

Bob started the twin 150 hp Yamaha engines, letting them

warm up while he helped Michelle on board and seated her on the padded bench attached to the front of the console. As they slowly moved through the inlet, the strong odors of the dock area reminded Michelle of many previous boat trips; the smell of freshly cleaned fish, commingled with gasoline and creosote, and the earthy raw odor of the nearby marsh and mud flats. It was strangely pleasant, even romantic.

She sat back and enjoyed the trip out, sipping on the can of Budweiser Bob proffered. She had been looking forward to this as a diversion from the constant grind of the case, which had been wearing on both her and Rick. She was also secretly excited to see Craig again, and was relieved that Rick was not jealous.

Meeting Dr. Cindy Matthews and her husband was another incentive, and she knew Craig had purposefully arranged that to make sure she would come. Ah, the privileges and persuasions of a billionaire! Dr. Matthews was a leading expert in the psychological assessments of serial murders and worked with the DC police. Craig had flown her down to help with the case but first—pleasure before business—was hosting them all on a cruise off the coast.

Fishermen on the flanking jetties waved to her as they exited the inlet. Once past the NO WAKE buoys, Bob said, "Hold on, m'am," and cranked the throttle forward. The bow lifted off the water, angling upwards, and as the engines reached cruising speed, the boat settled onto a horizontal plane, the deep-V hull slicing through the light swells with sibilant sighs.

They passed other boats of varying makes and sizes; few could match the speed of the Wellcraft in these conditions, and the captain longed to unleash the full power of the engines and see if he could top 70. But his orders were to bring the guests out with "comfortable speed," so he kept it to thirty knots and enjoyed the ride, and the pretty lady, who leaned back against the console and let the wind plaster her dress to her body.

With some effort he redirected his gaze to the horizon. He pointed ahead and announced, "There she is, m'am!"

Michelle had noticed the yacht shortly after leaving the jetty, but she had assumed it was a cruise ship! "Why do you call boats 'she,'" she asked Bob.

He laughed and nodded toward the yacht. "A boat that beautiful could never be called 'he.' The Russians call their boats 'he,' but what do they know? No, there's something feminine about boats and ships, their grace and subtle power. The way they get you where you need to go. The way you ride them. No wonder men fall in love with boats as much as they do women.

She turned and looked up at him with surprise. "Why Capt. Bob, you're a poet disguised as a boat captain. What a lovely tribute to women *and* boats."

He laughed. "I'm glad I didn't add the sexist part," he winked. "That both can run you aground and cost you a pile of money.

They approached the yacht— 157 feet from bow to stern, 35 feet from the waterline to the top of the radar mast, three decks, a Jacuzzi, formal dining room and accommodations for 12. Jet skis, snorkeling gear, kayaks, bikes and a 20-foot inflatable for going dockside. She was a floating pleasure palace, capable of going anywhere in the world. Hansen had been to just about every continent on her, including Antarctica.

She was anchored in 40 feet of water, and lit up like a radioactive Christmas tree in Times Square, sparkling like a white diamond. Beethoven's Pastoral Symphony greeted their arrival as Bob secured his boat to the aft docking platform. As she stepped over to the big boat, aided by a khaki-clad crewmember, Michelle noticed the name, written in twelve-inch gold letters: Glasnost.

Four of the yacht's crewmembers boarded Bob's boat. As he pulled away, Bob waved to Michelle, saying, "Have fun. I'll see you later tonight."

Michelle waved back and watched them speed away. The sun was getting low, she luxuriated in the sounds and smells of the twilight sea. She climbed the short ladder to the main deck. Craig Hansen stood waiting, his hand extended to help her into the cockpit. She was struck by his elegant charisma, even in a golf shirt, shorts and boat shoes. She smiled and accepted his hand.

"Welcome aboard The *Glasnost*."

"That means 'open government' in Russian, right? Why would you choose a Russian word for the name of your boat?"

"My mother was Russian."

A chill passed through her before she entered the air-conditioned cabin. He poured her a glass of Cristal, showing her the label. "Only the best for you, Michelle. Only the best"

She shivered as Hansen toasted her.

"To art!"

34

August 1, 7:52 p.m.

Second Precinct, VBPD

Virginia Beach

Ordberg assembled his team in the meeting room they had commandeered early in the investigation; it was filled with maps, reports, documents and photos related to the case, all obsessively organized and labeled per the Dapper Detective, John Ordberg.

Tonya sat at one table with three laptops and two uniformed officers, working various online leads, continuing to run down information from the FBI database. Ordberg and Rick were at another table working a bank of phones. In an interrogation room down the hall, the security guard, Ritz camera manager and Russian model, overseen by Wheels Johnson, were pouring over hundreds of photos of Hospitality America employees.

Ordberg finished his phone conversation.

"Listen up. That was Jacobs over at the Hospitality America garage. The van was signed out from the garage June 19 by a V. Wilson. No such person exists, according to their employment records. The manager says the guy had proper ID and clearance. Said he had a beard. Jacobs showed him the sketch of the pier perp—same guy. Thoughts?"

"It would probably have to be an employee to fake the ID, and to know the procedures for checking out the van," offered Rick.

"Or someone who paid an employee a lot of money to get the card issued," replied Tonya.

The door opened and Wheels rolled into the room. "Bad news, Loo. The witnesses have been through all the employee photos. We got a big zero."

"Have them look again."

"They've been through them three times, Loo. We got nothing. Our guy doesn't work for the hotels."

Ordberg stood and walked to the door. "Well, shit fire!"

Rick applauded, following Ordberg out, saying, "Well done, Loo. Try using 'tarnation' and 'dad blasted' next time for *real* punch!"

They walked out to the lobby, where Wheels had assembled the three witnesses. While they were parting company, the model with nine lives, Marena Fedotova, put her hand over her mouth and pointed over Rick's shoulder, a horrified expression on her face. She backed away, speaking in Russian, shaking her head. They all turned to look at the TV.

"Holy shit, that's him!" said Jeremy Wilson, the pier security guard. They all walked closer to the TV, where a press conference that had been taped earlier in the day was being broadcast on a local channel.

"Yeah, I think so, too," said Bob Smith, the Ritz Camera manager. "It's his mouth for sure. Yeah, the eyes, too."

"Which guy are you talking about?" asked Rick. There were several men and a few women in the shot, one at the podium and the rest behind or to the side. The screen changed to a close-up of the man speaking at the podium. Marena screamed, turned frantically and ran directly into the wall, where she stayed, moaning and rocking herself, mumbling and seemingly praying in Russian.

The man who elicited this primal reaction was none other than the billionaire owner of Hospitality America, Craig Hansen.

"Oh shit!" cried Rick, grabbing for his phone. There was a voice mail message flashing from Michelle and he listened to it, all eyes on him; his face went white, his expression shocked.

Ordberg grabbed his arm. "What is it, Rick?"

"John, Michelle's on Hansen's boat. She's out there alone with him!"

35

August 1, 8:32 p.m.

Onboard *The Glasnost*

Atlantic Ocean

MICHELLE WAS WORKING ON HER second drink and starting to relax, her earlier reaction written off to nerves. Hansen had given her a tour of his boat: the bridge with its complex navigation equipment, the small gym with a compact and complete set of machines and gear, the salon, galley and decks and—finally—the staterooms.

Michelle was admiring the many paintings and prints that lined the companionways. She was not surprised that a few were original Picasso prints. Impressed, but not surprised.

"Let me show you another painting, Michelle, and see if you can recognize the artist." He led her into the last stateroom where, taking up the entire space above the king-size bed, was a beautiful landscape of a town on a hill with a river flowing by.

After studying it for a while, Michelle said, "I don't recognize this one. It reminds me of some of the work I've seen from the 19th century French painters, but who knows? Masterfully done. Who painted it?"

"I did," replied Craig, sounding pleased with himself. "I attended VCU's art program for a year, thought I was going to be the next Modigliani."

"What happened? Why did you stop?"

"Life happened. I took a job the summer after my sophomore year at my uncle's hotel and I was hooked. There was something so grand about running a hotel and it got into my blood. Turns out I was quite good at it, as you can see."

"Do you still paint?"

"Oh, a little bit here and there. I like to think that now my life is my canvas."

Their eyes met, and again she felt the icy warning in her bloodstream. This time she paid attention.

"Let's go on deck, Craig. I've caught a chill down here." He led the way out and up to the sun deck. She checked her phone again for calls. No signal; they were too far out. "Craig, could I use the ship's phone to call Rick?"

"I'm sorry, Michelle, but the system is down. Happened on the way out. Would you like me to radio the station?"

"No, but I'm just worried about Rick getting out here."

"Capt. Bob will bring him and the others as soon as they arrive, I'm sure. Dr. Matthews was running late; we can expect them in about an hour."

"Where is the rest of your crew? I thought it took several to run this boat?"

"True, but we're anchored, Michelle. Quite safe and easy, even for a billionaire!" He laughed easily, his back to her, as he surreptitiously poured a vial of liquid into her drink. He handed it to her with another toast, "To Michelle, a priceless work of art!"

She laughed and said, "Tell me about your Russian mother."

His expression darkened. "She lives in Russia. I hardly know her."

"But why?"

"My father was a diplomat with the State Department and met my mother while he was in Moscow. They fell in love, married and he brought her home. I came along a few years later. When I was six she left. Never said goodbye, no reason, just left. I found out later she had cleaned out the bank account to the tune of $500,000—pretty big money back then."

"Oh, that's terrible, Craig. What a shame for your family. How did your father deal with it?"

"He committed suicide a year later. I was seven years old and an orphan. My dad's brother took me in and I grew up with my aunt and uncle here at the Beach. He's the one who launched my career in hotels."

Michelle yawned and stretched out on the chaise lounge. "Wow, I can't keep my eyes open, Craig. Oh my, those drinks were strong." She tried to laugh but was rapidly growing weaker. In less than a minute she was asleep. Craig lifted her up over his shoulder and carried her down to his stateroom and laid her on the bed.

He pulled out a small suitcase holding several articles of women's clothing and a makeup kit. He smiled, looking down at his final piece of art. He knew they were onto him; he could feel it. What he was doing was foolish, but he didn't care anymore. It was all going south, but at least his art would survive and, in the end, that would redeem everything.

36

August 1, 8:53 p.m.

Dam Neck Annex

Virginia Beach

THANK GOD FOR THE FEDS, thought Ordberg for the fifth time. Elena Grigorevna had made a few calls to her superiors in DC and—after it was determined that a possible abduction was being carried out in federal waters—a SEAL team was dispatched from Dam Neck's Naval Special Warfare Development Group, or DEVGRU.

Normally that might have taken hours, depending on the training rotation, but Counterterrorism Team Five was on hand and ready. Two Fast-Attack inflatables had launched from Rudee Inlet, and the Blackhawk helicopters were about to lift off.

"DEVGRU," said Rick, as he and Ordberg tightened their

rappelling harnesses. "Sounds like the name of a metal band."

Lt. Camon laughed, and checked their gear. "You guys are good to go. You must have some friends on high, cause we don't let just anybody slip and slide. Just remember what I told you; you don't have to do anything. We've got your harness set for a slow rate of descent. You'll feel like a rock, but trust me, you're not. Flex and bend, you know the rest. And let our guys unhook you. Keep your helmets on even when we land, so you can hear our signals. We lead, you follow. Got it?"

Rick and Ordberg nodded and followed Camon and the rest of the team over to the Blackhawk helicopter that was spooling up fifty yards away. Within a minute, the entire team and their gear were secured on board and the chopper was lifting off. One of the team grabbed a laptop and brought up the image of a large yacht on a mounted display.

"Gentlemen," came the voice of Master Chief Ron Davis through the helmet earpieces. He pointed at the display. "Our target is *The Glasnost*, a 157-foot yacht. Three decks, top speed 30 knots. According to SATCOM, she is currently anchored." Schematics of the decks came up on screen. "We will go in fast and high; drop point is the sun deck. Three decks, three teams, you know who you are. The boats will arrive simultaneously and will cover escape attempts and sea assaults."

He pointed toward Rick and Jameson. "The cops are with Camon."

Three photos of Hansen filled the screen. "Our target is Mr. Craig Hansen. Gentlemen, he has murdered five people and is a hostile. Armed and dangerous. He's holding a hostage, a Michelle Paige." Two photos of Michelle came up, followed by whistles from some of the team. "Stow that, she belongs to Mr. Jameson."

"Going up, boys. Hang on!" said the pilot as he put the

chopper into a steep climb, quickly gaining altitude.

"Are we clearing airspace?" asked Rick of Davis.

"No, we're coming in vertical, from a very steep angle. People tend to look for choppers low and level, not swooping down on them from above. Increases the element of surprise."

"So what if he has radar on board and other early warning devices?"

"Oh, we know he has radar. Any boat that size would be fitted with a sophisticated system. We're showing up clear as day right now, if he's looking. Since we're climbing away from him, I doubt it."

Within five minutes they were at 5,000 feet and in position for the attack, about half a mile east of the boat. The pilot brought the bird around and said, "In position, Chief. Oops, hang on....target is moving, turning east...yeah, fast turns, Chief. She's in a hurry."

"Take her down," replied Davis. The deck tilted as the pilot put the Blackhawk into a steep circling dive that would put them on the deck in about a minute. The team tightened up their harnesses and double-checked their gear and weapons.

Camon tugged Rick and Ordberg's harnesses tighter and checked them out again. "You guys good to go?"

"I need to go potty," said Rick, deadpan.

"You'll just have to hold it, sir," he whispered to Rick.

The boat was getting rapidly larger as the pilot flared for landing. The sound was deafening as it reflected off of the ocean and the boat. Suddenly a figure appeared on the upper deck and lifted a large gun to his shoulder.

"Gun, gun, gun!" yelled the pilot, taking evasive action as the rounds slammed into the armored hull of the Blackhawk, sounding like microwaved popcorn. The pilot side slipped aft of the shooter and hovered just above the main deck launching platform. Camon threw out the rappelling line and steadied it as each team member clipped on and disappeared into the blackness. Within five seconds all were down and Camon was grabbing Rick and then Ordberg, clipping them to the lines, putting their hands on the brake and shoving them out the door. He followed closely behind. In less than thirty seconds the entire team was on the boat, the chopper rapidly moving away to circle at altitude in case it was needed later.

37

August 1, 9:26 p.m.

On board *The Glasnost*

Atlantic Ocean

HANSEN HAD JUST LAID OUT all his painting supplies when his iPhone proximity alert alarm went off. He had tied it into the onboard wireless system, and if anything went wrong with the engines, onboard systems or, as in this case, if his radar reported a proximity threat of a boat or aircraft, he would know. The system was expensive, but priceless. His display said AIRCRAFT ALERT!

Damn, that was fast, he thought. Ordberg! They figured it out faster than he had planned, but he was ready. He had been born ready. He looked down once more at the sleeping Michelle, now completely nude and chained to his bed. What a beauty she is. What a piece of art she would have made but, alas, she would now have to be pyro art.

He moved to another cabinet and placed his hand on a glass pad. It scanned his palm print and retracted a door to reveal a full cache of weapons and gear. He put on a lightweight kevlar vest, knowing that the SEALS would go for a body shot unless they had him zeroed and still.

Why not give them a proper welcome, he thought, grabbing the Uzi submachine gun and five clips. He grabbed a Beretta 9mm pistol and three clips and five small cylinders about ten inches long, with an elastic strap attached. All except the Uzi went into a small black backpack.

Lastly, he took out his keys and used an unusual red one to open a small panel built flush inside the wall of the cabinet. It was labeled "D-Day." Inside was another palm scanner and a keypad. He flipped the switch to ARMED and set the timer for 10:00. It began a digital countdown that would end with 50 pounds of plastic explosives blowing his boat—and anyone unlucky enough to be onboard—to bits.

As he raced to the upper decks he could make out the sound of the chopper's rotors, still some distance above him, but rapidly descending. Military! Even better, he thought. Let them come and finish the job Ordberg and his punks could not. Ha, it took the might of the United States military to take down the likes of Sergei the Terrible. Not the Virginia Beach Police Department. Not the FBI. The United States Fucking Military!

By the time he reached the bridge deck the roar of the chopper filled the air, and the boat was literally shaking from the beat of the rotors; but he was not afraid. He calmly stepped out from the bridge, pointed the Uzi, and emptied a clip into the chopper. It moved aft of him, partially hidden by the upper deck wings, radar tower and other equipment on the main mast.

By now he knew he was dealing with SEALS, and he had

little time if he wanted to end it on his terms. He had already decided he would not be taken. Better to die than be captured. His blood was coursing through his veins and the bloodlust was on him. Oh, how grand it would be to go down in a hail of bullets fired by Navy SEALS! What a wonderful way to be remembered and to exit this life. All he had to do was take off the vest and welcome their bullets.

Or live on. He could, if he chose to. His hand absently stroked one of the stainless steel cylinders, a re-breather that would give him ten minutes of underwater breathing; five would give him nearly an hour underwater; plenty of time to hide and hopefully escape. As he contemplated his next move, he could hear the SEAL team moving toward him, below and above deck. He could also hear their support boats, probably fast-attack support inflatables. But they couldn't spot him yet where he squatted near the bow.

He waited until he saw a shape rise up from the darkness near the bridge, stood and fired two quick shots with his pistol, holding his position. As expected, several shots were returned, four of them hitting him on the vest, the force pushing him back. His arms windmilled as he tried to keep his balance, but he tripped on the short side railing and fell over the side of the boat.

The shock of the fall was harder than he had expected, and he bounced along the surface a few times from the forward momentum, then remembered to let his body go limp, knowing they would be watching through their night-vision goggles.

"Target down, target down! Man overboard!"

Within moments the SEAL team had secured the boat, reduced the speed and brought it around to the approximate position where Hansen had fallen overboard. The chopper was circling, using a searchlight on the water around the boat, and the two fast-attack boats were also circling and searching for the target's body.

They found Michelle alive, and Rick and two of the SEALS worked to remove the chains. The padlocks resisted all their attempts to open them; they didn't have the proper tools to break them. She was just starting to wake up from the cocktail Hansen had given her. Rick covered her up and sat beside her for the boat ride back to shore.

On deck, Chief Davis and Ordberg were questioning the team member who had shot Hansen.

"I definitely hit him, sir," said Jenkins.

"Tell me exactly what happened," ordered Davis.

"He popped off about four shots at me, sir, from near the bow. Then I returned fire. Five shots. He cried out, stood, kind of staggered and then fell off the boat, sir."

"Did you see where you hit him?"

"No sir, the muzzle blasts blinded me."

"Okay, good work, Jenkins. Go work with Camon and the boats."

He turned to Ordberg and gestured out to the water. "Well, Lieutenant, good news and bad news. The gunsight cameras confirmed the hits. Looked like he was hit by three or four rounds. So unless he was wearing a vest, he's dead or will be soon. Chances are 50/50 we'll find the body this far out. These currents are close enough to the Gulf Stream that they really move, plus the vertical currents are significant, so a body out here can get sucked down and stay down for a long time. And if it stays down that long, usually there ain't much left when it comes back up."

"What's the good news?" asked Ordberg.

"Problem solved. Your bad guy is out of the picture."

"Yeah, but is he dead?"

"If he can survive bullets, falling off a boat going 30 knots and manage to stay afloat in the ocean, losing blood without getting eaten by a shark, then he must be one lucky son of a bitch."

"I wonder," replied Ordberg.

They both turned at the sound of running feet from below deck. Soon the entire team burst out of the cabin.

"Sir, we've got an armed detonator with about two minutes on it! We've called in the boats. We gotta get lost, fast!"

Rick came out a minute later. "John, we can't get Michelle out. We have to find the bombs."

"There's no time, Rick."

"Bullshit. We have to save her! I'm going back in."

"Stop him," barked Davis, and two SEALS quickly immobilized Rick, tied his wrists with zip ties and threw him onto one of the boats. The others quickly followed. Rick continued to fight and scream until Davis ordered one of the team to "put him asleep." Rick was knocked out for the duration.

They were only a quarter-mile away when the boat exploded: three charges going off within two seconds. The first was near the bow, which lifted off the water and plunged straight down into the ocean. The second and third were amidships, which tore the ship in half. Within five seconds the fuel tank, with more than 2,500 gallons of high-octane diesel, exploded, sending a huge fireball overhead that lit the sky and could be seen for many miles in all directions.

The concussive force of the explosion knocked two SEALS off one of the inflatables, and knocked everyone else over or down into the gunnels. They watched the spectacular apocalypse before them. The yacht's two sections began sinking in the middle, creating a V-shaped tomb for Michelle Paige's body.

And then it was gone, the night dark again except for pools of burning fuel that floated on the ocean surface, hissing and flickering in the water.

38

August 2, 4:34 a.m.

Off Corolla Beach

Atlantic Ocean

IT HAD BEEN SO SURPRISINGLY EASY, thought Hansen, as he watched the fishing boat approach, guided by his hand-held beacon. Yes, Lady Luck was definitely on his side tonight.

After purposely falling off his boat, his backpack had been nearly ripped away from him. He had managed to hold onto one strap as he bounced across the waves and then settled down into the water. The weight of the kevlar vest took him down quickly, but he calmly reached under the vest and inflated his buoyancy compensator vest, neutralizing his descent, which leveled off about 15 feet beneath the surface.

He removed the re-breather from the bag and strapped it on, breathing the compressed air. He put on the small flippers he'd packed and started swimming rapidly south with the current, trying to put as much distance between himself and the explosion. The sounds of his ship's screws and the whine of the smaller inflatable boats faded behind him, though the chopper's bass whup-whup-whup continued for some time, ever warning him to dive deeper to avoid the sweeping spotlight.

After he finished his second tank of air, he estimated he was about a mile from the boat; he surfaced and looked back. It was like a scene from a movie: two choppers circling the boat, four fast boats also circling and making passes on a grid. They were searching outside of his location, so he was inside the box. He would have to be careful.

He had seen them evacuate the boat with about three minutes left. Hard to kill SEALS, he thought, as the boats and choppers retreated from his boat. Then he watched the countdown and waited for his boat to die. The explosions literally pushed him back under the water and took his breath away. He had to increase his vest's buoyancy as he fought to remain conscious.

He finished watching his boat come apart and then continued swimming south. He decided to save the air tanks and switch to snorkel and swim on the surface. It was more dangerous that way, but also faster, and his air supply would last longer. When one of the choppers or boats headed his way he simply strapped on the re-breather and descended until they had passed, then headed back up to the surface, stowed the re-breather and continued south. He was in excellent shape, but his muscles were beginning to cramp and he knew that soon he would have to rest longer and swim less.

In this cat-and-mouse manner he made his way slowly south and out of the box, aided by the current and the tide, using all but one of his tanks until now, when the fishing boat spotted him five miles off Corolla beach. They had a hand-held spot on him and he waved.

The captain throttled down and came alongside so that the mate could hand him a boat hook. He grabbed it and the mate pulled him around to the stern, where the gunnels were the lowest. He opened the fishing hatch and pulled him into the boat like a landed marlin.

"You are one lucky hombre," remarked the mate, as he helped Craig sit up and handed him a towel. He pointed north to where distant searchlights still played across the waters off Virginia Beach. "You have anything to do with that search?"

"Yeah, but I don't think they know about me. I had pulled alongside that huge yacht when it blew up. Knocked me right on my ass and a piece of shrapnel came down and tore a big-assed hole in my boat. She sank right out from under me. It was gone in less than a minute."

"No shit? Well ain't that some bad luck. Let me go tell the captain so we can call it in to the Coast Guard."

Craig was more tired than he had ever been, but he knew he needed to move fast and take control of the situation. Finally, he got the strength to dig through his pack and pull the Beretta out from the waterproof case. He slid in a full clip and racked a round into place. He slowly stood, got his balance, and walked toward the wheelhouse, where the captain was on the radio.

"Coast Guard, Coast Guard, this is fishing boat Tanager 2 off of Corolla, do you copy?"

"Put down the mic!" ordered Craig, his gun on the captain and the first mate. Both turned to him, incredulous looks on their faces.

"The hell you say," said the captain. "We just saved your life and now you pull a gun on me on <u>my</u> boat?"

The radio blared to life. "Tanager 2, this is Coast Guard Elizabeth City, we copy. State your problem."

The captain keyed the mic and started to speak. Craig shot him in the head, then walked up to the motionless and shell-shocked mate and shot him between the eyes, point blank.

"Tanager 2, this is the Coast Guard Elizabeth City, was that gunfire? Do you need assistance?"

Craig grabbed the microphone from the floor, untangled the cord from around the captain's arm and replied, using a perfect imitation of the captain, "Coast Guard Elizabeth City, this is Tanager 2, that was an engine backfire, but she's running good now. Looks like we won't need a tow, boys! Sorry for the bother. Copy?"

"Tanager 2, this is Coast Guard, copy you do not need assistance. Be advised of a military security alert in effect ten miles north of you. What is your destination?"

"Manteo. Then the Bahamas."

The sound of laughter drifted in from Elizabeth City. "Roger that, Tanager 2. Copy Manteo and Bahamas. Better catch a lot of fish! This is the U.S. Coast Guard Elizabeth City, out."

Craig weighted the bodies down and tossed them overboard, then washed the deck and cabin with the onboard hose, removing all signs of foul play. He dressed in the clothes he had taken off the mate, and assumed the role of a fishing boat captain. He had enough fuel for South Carolina, where he could buy a faster boat.

Then the Bahamas. After all, the Coast Guard was expecting him.

EPILOGUE

August 10, 2:51 p.m.

VBPD Second Precinct

Virginia Beach

JOHN ORDBERG STROLLED INTO Capt. Roger's office, looking resplendent as usual, with a Cheshire smile on his face. "You wanted to see me, sir?"

"What are _you_ smilin' about, John?"

"Oh nothing, sir. Just thinking about how I'm going to spend my winnings from last night's game."

"Kiss my ass, Loo! I was gonna use that money for a new boat motor." He pointed to a chair, and Ordberg sat. Rogers pulled three photos from a file on his desk and handed them over.

"Those are photos taken of a bottle that washed up down on Carolina Beach day before yesterday."

"The label's been washed off, but clearly this is a Cristal bottle."

"You sure know how to ruin a good surprise, John. Yeah, it's a Cristal bottle and there was a note inside. From your friend Craig Hansen." He handed a transcription of the note to Ordberg.

"We're not friends, Captain."

"Well, he seems to think so. Read it."

The note was on the same hand-made deckled paper as the others left at the scenes of the three murders, with the same flowing, elegant script.

"Forensics matched the handwriting. It's Hansen's," added Rogers as Ordberg read:

> *Lt. John Ordberg,*
> *Virginia Beach Police Department*
> *Special Victims Unit*

> *"Salutations my friend,*

> *You were on my mind and my heart when I wrote this letter. You have been a worthy adversary, but unfortunately not worthy enough. Always a step behind, John. But I do concede that you dress well and you look good. I am very sorry that I broke your success record but alas, our destiny together was such that you would never catch me alive.*

> *As I write this I have not decided if I*

will live or die, but either way the end result will be spectacular and a work of art. If you do not find my body, there is a very good chance that we will see each other again, perhaps sooner than you think. After all, art never dies. And neither do I. I shall never forget you, John, and I know you will never forget me.

Craig

PS- Tell your friend Rick I think about Michelle every day.

"Fucking asshole," said Ordberg.

"Wow, strong language from the Loo."

"I'm not afraid of this guy, Len. Neither is Rick."

"I know, John. But even so, you guys keep your eyes open, and watch your six. I got a feeling this guy's not dead. Now get out of here and go catch some bad guys."

"Aye, sir," replied Ordberg, and walked out of the office, the Cheshire grin now replaced with the look of a hungry predator.

Read all three Virginia Beach Murder Mysteries.

Available in print on Amazon and Barnes & Noble, and in epub on Kindle, Nook and iBooks.
www.beachmurdermysteries.com

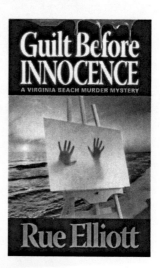

CPSIA information can be obtained at www.ICGtesting.com
Printed in the USA
LVOW052033300712

292200LV00001B/3/P